Hall

of

Heroes

With thanks

to Martha Jenkins

Contents

Chapter One: Search for Adventure

 When Mr. Orlando asked for volunteers in the church's Young Helps program, I volunteered. Mom said I could. Young Helps was a program to bring church kids into the homes of elderly people to help with the housework and things like that. But I didn't get an elderly person. You could say that this book is about what I did get.

Nobody else in the family volunteered. Rebecca's my oldest sister, and she used to be a lot of fun before she started high school. She would make up mystery stories for me or take me with her to the shopping center around the corner. But as soon as she got into high school, she made friends with Suzette, and at night she had Spanish to work on.

Curtis and Rebecca are twins (fraternal twins, they insist on telling people.) Curt's too quick and bouncy to stop long enough to do housework for anybody, let alone people he doesn't know.

I come after Curt and Rebecca, and--really--I was underage for the Young Helps program. Kids were supposed to be at least twelve. But in case you have any doubts, I'll tell you up front--I am extremely well behaved and responsible. I've never done anything out of the ordinary. When I asked Mr. Orlando if I could sign up for Young Helps he said that--- seeing as it was me---he'd make an exception.

"In fact," he told me, "I have just the person for you. Yes-- this timing is from the Lord, Jean. I nearly had to tell Martha--Miss Harris, that is--that I couldn't find anybody suitable. I think you'll do just fine."

That remark right there let me know that this Martha Harris was different somehow. He'd been holding back her assignment for some reason.

He gave me her address and phone number. Everybody on the list to get a helper was a church member in good standing, who had interviewed with Pastor and had become acquainted with the Young Helps program before being allowed on the list. I went home and showed the address to Mom and Dad.

Mom was making salad for dinner when I came in, and Dad was at the kitchen table, slicing onions for her because onions make her cry. She stopped long enough to glance at the card with the name and address on it. "Martha Harris," she said. She glanced at Dad. "Now isn't that odd." She said it more like a statement than a question.

"How's that?" he asked.

"Maybe I'm thinking of the wrong person. Do you know her?" Mom asked.

He glanced up at her. "Sure, honey, you've seen her--Southern woman. Georgia accent. I think her parents attended our church a long time ago when they were still alive."

"Yes, that's who I thought. She's retired here, I believe. I'll give her a call tonight. It's all right, of course. I just hadn't expected her to be on the list." Dad didn't seem to be too concerned about it, and Mom's curiosity didn't last much longer. I had no idea who she was, and since neither one of them thought to explain to me that Martha Harris wasn't elderly, I just supposed that she was.

"Curt says there's a meeting tonight at the Hall of Heroes," Dad called after me. "You'd better hurry, because I think they're out there already."

"Okay." I ran to my room and changed from my school clothes into regular clothes, got my boots and gloves and things, and hurried outside. Curt and Rebecca had formed their own society, called the Hall of Heroes. They both read Beowulf for school, and they said that a long time ago, heroes always feasted each other in great halls. They immediately pulled Curt's best friend Digger in on it, because Digger is the absolute bravest, toughest, most heroic kid we know. But then of course we had to let Rebecca's best friend Suzette in on it. Then Curtis and Rebecca decided that the cut-off age for the Hall of Heroes was 13. And of course Suzette agreed with this and said I was way too young to join. But Digger took my side like he always does, and he said if I couldn't join then he wouldn't join either. So they agreed that I should join, but I didn't get to bring any of my friends into it.

Digger and Suzette both said it was too hard to call ourselves the Hall of Heroes Feasters, so the boys called themselves the Sword Bearers, and the girls called themselves the Shield Maidens, and when we all got together, the whole group would be called the Hall of Heroes, or just "the Hall" for short. And that name stuck. I didn't have much say on what titles we picked.

Dad owned a couple of empty lots a few streets over, and there was a metal storage shed on one of them. I had always called it our clubhouse, but Rebecca said clubhouses were for little kids. She said it would be our rendezvous point. Whenever the Sword Bearers and Shield Maidens were supposed to have a meeting for the Hall of Heroes, we would all rally at the rendezvous point. That did sound to me more like a Sword Bearer and Shield Maiden kind of thing to do. I mean, I couldn't imagine big hairy guys with horns on their helmets having a clubhouse. What would they do there? But I could imagine them rallying at a rendezvous point.

The rendezvous point was so small that when all five of us crammed into it we only had room to talk and lay plans. We couldn't even sit down. Digger had found an old wooden table, and it had been a narrow vote on allowing it inside, because it cramped us even more. Its surface only measured two and a half feet by two and a half feet, and some of the Shield Maidens looked upon it as nothing but a splintery way to give up some more space. However, it was voted in after a lot of discussion and some argument. Rebecca and Suzette got mad at me because I voted with Digger and Curtis to keep it. I didn't like the table, but I voted with Digger because he let me join.

One nice thing about the shed was that it had a wooden floor. Most of the metal sheds that you buy at garden shops have no floor at all. But Dad had put in a wooden floor and put it up on skids so that he could move the around as he needed to. We bargained with him to let us use it if we could find storage places for all the odds and ends that he'd kept in it. He agreed, and we cleaned out and re-packed our garage to make room for the extra stuff.

Now the day was ending. I hurried along as fast as I could without running. I didn't want to act like I was afraid they would go on and leave the rendezvous point without me, so I didn't want to run. My watch showed that it was only a little after four, but the sky overhead was already dim, and there was a border of red in the west, from the sunset. If there hadn't been snow everywhere it would have seemed kind of eerie. I don't like the dark. But the snow caught the faint glow from the street lights and the fainter glow from the dim and distant stars that were beginning to make an appearance.

I crossed the street from a line of neat houses and trotted into one of the empty lots, and I could see the rendezvous point, with light from somebody's battery lamp spilling through the narrow doorway. I didn't pay attention to anything around me. But suddenly somebody jerked real hard on my scarf from behind and pulled me down backward.

I landed plump! right on the ground.

The jerk had also cut off my wind for a second, so I couldn't even yell or say anything for a second.

"Hey girl, what're you doing in our lot?" A boy asked me. I was still sitting on the cold snow. I looked up, kind of blinking through my glasses, and saw that three boys were standing over me.

"We're talking to you, girl. This ain't your property."

"It's my dad's," I said.

"Liar!" One of the others exclaimed. He kicked snow on me.

"It is!" I told him. I pointed at the shed, which was easily visible from where we were. "My brother and sister are over there."

"Well they're in a lot of trouble for using our shed," the first one told me. "We put that up there."

"Now you're lying," I told him. "My dad put that up."

One of them grabbed me by my coat and pulled me right up to my feet. He shook me really hard, to scare me, I guess. It worked.

"Curt!" I yelled. "Digger!"

He threw me into one of his friends, but just then Digger' head popped out of the open doorway, and even from that distance I could hear him say to the others inside, "Hey, come on!"

They came streaming out of the shed, all four of them, all older than I am. I don't think that my three bullies bothered to see how many of the rescuers were boys and how many were girls. It must have looked to them like a whole group of kids just streamed right out of there, ready to fight. Digger was holding Smaxcaliber, our ax handle that doubled as a sword and mascot, but I don't think he was brandishing it as a threat. Digger always held Smaxcaliber during our meetings. But these three bullies didn't know that.

Anyway, the three boys who had stopped me ran off in the opposite direction, through the empty lot to the street, and then through the other yards until they were out of sight. Digger got to me first.

"What happened?" he asked. "Who were they?"

"Bullies," I told him. "They said I was trespassing."

"I think that tall one is Eddy Reinbach," Digger said. "We used to hang out together".

Curt and Rebecca came pounding up, and then Suzette.

"Sword Bearers to the rescue," Curt sang, panting. "Those kids roughing you up?"

"They wanted to," I said. "Thanks for coming."

"I think that's the same three who bombed us with snowballs this afternoon," Suzette told Rebecca. She glanced at her watch in the dimness and squinted at it. "It was less than an hour ago."

"Digger says one of them was Eddy Reinbach," I added.

Suzette instantly became indignant, like it was my fault. "Eddy Reinbach! Everybody knows he's no good! He steals everything he can. You shouldn't be talking to kids like Eddy Reinbach, Jean! If you were old enough to use your brains, you'd know how bad he is."

I opened my mouth to talk, but Digger said, "Come on, let's go back to the clubhouse."

"Rendezvous point," Rebecca exclaimed.

"Those three want to start trouble," I said. "They say it's their lot and their shed. I think we should get ready for them." But nobody even paid attention to my comment.

Chapter Two: Meeting of the Hall of Heroes

The rendezvous point was furnished with nothing more than the small and splintery table. At that moment, Digger' battery powered lamp sat on top of the table, and alongside it lay Smaxcaliber, our axe handle that doubled as a sword and mascot for the Hall of Heroes. Other than that the room was empty and cold. The thin metal walls didn't insulate at all.

But with the light shining up on our faces as we crammed our way inside, it was easy to feel like this was a mysterious place, and like adventures were waiting for us everywhere. "Who has news?" Digger asked.

"I do," I said.

"Say on, Berwyn," he invited me. Berwyn is my name in the Hall of Heroes. I always forget that and answer to Jean in our meetings, but Digger reminds me.

"I volunteered to join Young Helps on Sunday," I said confidently. "I got assigned to a woman named Martha Harris."

Curtis groaned. "Jean! For crying out loud! What's that got to do with the Hall of Heroes!" he exclaimed. "We're looking for adventure!"

"No, Curt, that's the same woman you were asking me about at church!" Rebecca exclaimed.

"The one that looks so weird?" Curt asked, startled.

"What do you mean weird?" I asked. "Weird how?"

"Not weird," Rebecca said soothingly. "Just-- different. Like a big tall ghost or something."

"My dad says she's a recluse," Suzette volunteered. "She lives in the poor section on the very edge of town--a big wooden house that always has the draperies closed."

"What's a recluse?" I asked.

"Like a hermit, only a girl," Curt told me.

"Curt, a recluse can be either a boy or a girl!" Digger exclaimed. He glanced at me. "A recluse lives alone in a city and a hermit lives alone out in the country. And she can't really be a recluse if she goes to church."

"Well, maybe she's sick so she doesn't get out much," I said. I pictured a very tall, very old and bent over woman. "Maybe she's hard of hearing so she can't talk to people well."

"Maybe she locks kids up in her basement," Curt added. "Maybe she eats them."

"Stop it, Curt!" Digger exclaimed.

For a minute Curt actually did scare me when he talked about a lonely old woman locking kids up in her cellar. I knew exactly which house Suzette had been talking about, and it seemed like a house that would have a huge, dark, cavernous cellar. But instead of showing that I was scared, I said optimistically, "Well, maybe this Martha Harris has got an attic we could explore or old stuff we could use."

"I knew you were too young for the Hall of Heroes," Curt complained.

Rebecca interrupted him. "Cool it, Curtis. We're all in the Hall of Heroes."

"Well said," Digger agreed.

"Very well said," Suzette added. "We all entered the Hall of Heroes together." Suzette had a good reason to agree with that in front of the boys. Neither Digger nor Curt had wanted her to join at first. Suzette thinks about boys and talks about romance and stuff like that. It bugs Digger and Curt, but especially Digger.

"Okay, okay," Curtis said. "I'm sorry, Jean--I mean, Berwyn."

"That's okay, Eric," I said. Eric is Curtis's Sword Bearer name.

"If adventure beckons at Martha Harris's, Berwyn, let us know," Digger told me.

There was no other business to discuss, and it was getting close to five. "Since it's Friday," Digger told us, "That doughty matron of the hearth and home, my grandmother, has invited the Hall of Heroes in for an after dinner feast."

That was the nice way to say it. Digger lived with his grandmother, and he usually bargained with her to let us come over sometimes. If he shoveled enough snow for her or found enough extra work to do around the house, she would agree to something he wanted. She was nice enough to talk to, but we all knew we had to behave at his house or he would get into lots of trouble.

"What's the feast tonight?" Curtis asked.

"Chocolate cake from the market, if you guys can each kick in a dollar."

Everybody nodded and started pulling off their gloves to find their money. We liked going to Digger's house because he didn't have any little brothers or sisters to bother us. But we usually had to chip in if we wanted anything. We passed him our money.

"Well, this is one Sword Bearer who will be making tracks in your direction," Curtis told him.

Suzette and Rebecca went one way, to cut through yards and streets to get to Suzette's. Digger, Curtis and I went another way, around the block to Digger' house to leave him and his gear off.

"I wonder if those three guys that ganged up on us will try to stake out our lot and clubhouse," Curtis said.

"They say it's their club house," I reminded him.

"Rendezvous point!" Digger exclaimed. Then he added, "I hope not, but Eddy's just aching for a fight." He glanced at me. "When do you start this Young Helps deal?"

"Tomorrow," I told him.

"Well, adventure pops up in all kinds of places. Keep your ears and eyes open. And watch out for Eddy and his pals. Don't come alone to the clubhouse-- rendezvous point-- if you can help it. They'd leave us alone, but they might get a real charge out of picking on you."

"They were pretty rough," I told him.

But I forgot about them pretty soon. After dinner we went over to Digger's house and had our feast and played Risk.

It started to snow that night as we left to go home, and everybody else decided it would be great to go sledding the next day. I felt kind of bad, because I had to go see Miss Harris and would miss out. But that was part of being brave. I had volunteered and would have to do it. I was almost a hundred percent sure that she didn't lock kids up in her basement.

Chapter Three: Martha Harris

 Miss Harris lived in an old and wooden part of town. That's the way it looked to me. All of the houses were made of wood, and they kind of had a leaned over, tired out, unpainted sort of look. The morning's new snow had freshened up the hedges and the curbsides, and even the streets had suffered little enough traffic to look clean and white. But the poor houses drooped one way or another, their blind windows covered with plain and drab curtains. It did seem like the sort of neighborhood where tall and spooky old ladies might just lock little kids in basements. I began to wish that I had asked Curtis or Digger to come with me.

She lived in the ninth house on her street, and even though I counted the mailboxes to make sure I walked up the correct driveway, I already knew which house was hers. It was about the spookiest one, but maybe that was because it was the most run down, and because it had been abandoned and empty for a long time. In fact, I had never even noticed when somebody had moved into it again. Some of the other houses were right at the street, but Miss Harris' house was set back at the end of a long, unshoveled path. I silently trudged up the narrow yard. The walk made me feel more isolated.

I climbed the creaky steps and knocked on the door, and then waited for what seemed a long time. While I stood there, I looked back out towards the street and the silent neighborhood. It must have been one of the town's main streets once. Though old and worn, the houses had bay windows, and one or two had turrets on the second floor. Maybe in the spring if flowers were put out on the lawns the rows of houses would look pleasant. But now they looked like nobody cared.

I waited and waited, and at last I decided that I ought to go home and try next Saturday. It was sort of a relief because the house seemed to be getting bigger and droopier by the minute, like a lonely and hungry thing looming over me. But just as I turned to go, the heavy front door of the house opened inward.

Through the patched screen door I saw a woman who wasn't an old woman. She was tall and very white. Her face looked like there was a transparent layer of skin over it. That's how white she was. But her eyes looked dark.

"I've come to help Miss Martha Harris," I said in a small voice. "Is she home?"

"I am Martha Harris," she said, and I noticed that she had an accent. Not strong, but I could tell from the way she said her name---*Mah-tha*. She was southern, or had been, anyway.

She opened the screen door slowly and took a look at me. "You must be Jean. Please come inside."

For a moment I really didn't want to. For one thing, I was surprised that she was the woman I was supposed to help, because she was not an old woman. She looked like she was as young as my own mother, who was forty years old. She was tall, all right, and there was something about her--the long, draping robe that she wore, the ghostly complexion that she had. She looked very tired, and what made it worse was that she smiled at me and tried to act as though she wasn't tired. Even her lips were pale: not red, not pink, just a dull flesh color.

I stared up at her as I walked inside. I wondered why somebody her age would need a Young Helps person. I didn't realize it, but I kept looking at her as I walked past her inside the entrance of the house. At last she said, "I promise you, my dear, I won't bite you."

"Are you the only Martha Harris who lives here?" I asked. "I was sent for an old one. I mean, an elderly one. Like your mother, maybe."

"My mother doesn't live here anymore, Jean. She passed away several years ago. And besides, her name was Susan. Let me take your coat."

Miss Martha Harris was wearing a robe and slippers even though it was after one o'clock. She took my coat and hung it in the closet by the front door, and then she led me inside the old house. It was very old, very dusty, very silent and full of echoes. The floorboards were dark, dark brown. Instead of carpeting, there were heavy rugs everywhere. And the staircase in the center of the house had dark wooden steps. The railing was also heavy wood, darkly painted.

"I told Mr. Orlando that if you could handle the vacuuming and dusting, I could probably take care of the bathrooms. Do you mind doing dishes?" she asked.

"No, ma'am," I whispered.

"They accumulate so quickly. I think sometimes that elves must come in and dirty them while I sleep." And she laughed a slow and quiet laugh at her own joke.

I wasn't sure I liked her, though I did like her accent. But she didn't drawl or talk with a twang. Her voice, like the rest of her, was subdued, slow, and sort of droopy. Though she was tall for a woman, she didn't walk in strides. She kind of strolled, her hands in the side pockets of the robe, each elbow bent, her shoulders sloped forward. She may have been tall, but she wasn't big, not at all big, neither in the sense of being fat nor in the sense of being strong. She really did look like a tall, ghostly sort of woman. And she lived in an old, ghostly sort of house. We walked past the cellar door, and I wondered where they had buried her mother. But I squelched that thought.

I didn't want to be led around that long and dim house, but she showed me around the first floor. There was a kitchen at one end, with a dining room alongside it. But the dining room table was covered-- and I mean covered--with papers and books and a computer. Even the keyboard had papers all over it. I thought that maybe she must be an untidy person, but my conscience made me stop there. It wasn't right not to like her after only a few minutes.

Alongside the dining room was the stairway, but we didn't go up there. Instead, she took me into the small living room, where the floor was covered with a very heavy, square rug. The furniture was old and also heavy. It was like a house from long ago. Furniture from long ago.

"It is a bit too ornate for my tastes," she said as she saw me glance around at everything. "And dark, but it is a quiet place. My room is back here."

She took me to a room that must have been a porch once, but it was now paneled, with only a few windows, and there was a bed at one end of it, not made up. The room was long and narrow, and the floor was bowed. I wondered what in the world was upstairs. Why was her bedroom down here? But I told myself that maybe Miss Harris was afraid of fires at night. Some people use kerosene heaters in cold weather and are nervous about them, so they don't sleep upstairs.

"You can start to work today, if you like," she said.

I nodded. "That'll be fine."

"I'll show you where I keep my cleaning supplies."

She did, and I started out dusting. At home on Saturday mornings my mom will usually roll Rebecca and Curtis and me out of bed to help with cleaning. But when we clean, everybody cleans. However, at Miss Harris's, I cleaned, and she went back to her bedroom.

I dusted the whole first floor except the dining room table. On that, I dusted the top layers of papers, books, and other paraphernalia. But I didn't dare to move anything around. She didn't come out to tell me what else to do, so I just took it on myself to wash the sink full of dishes, and then I vacuumed. It was two thirty by then.

I decided that it was time to leave, but I didn't think it was polite just to walk out. I put away the vacuum cleaner and wandered back to the living room to find her seated on the couch.

"What a hard worker you are," she said.

I didn't know what to say to that because I was so surprised at how lazy she must be, so I just stumbled out with some silly answer like "yes," or "oh."

"Will you come back next week, Jean?" she asked. For the first time, we looked right at each other at the same time.

"Yes," I said, even though I didn't want to. I had kind of pictured in my mind that I would do housework for a nice old couple, and after I was finished they would sit and talk to me and we would become friends. That's what Young Helps was supposed to be for, so kids and older people could get to know each other.

Martha Harris could read people like people read books, and she knew right then that I didn't like her much. It wasn't until a lot later that I figured out that she'd known pretty much from the start what I was thinking.

All she did was look at me. Her look stopped me for a second--because it was deliberate, I guess. Maybe because it said some things that she didn't say, about giving her a chance. And I saw from it that she wanted to be friends with me.

"Is one o'clock on Saturday a good time?" I asked her.

"Fine." She took my hands and said thank you again. If I'd been older I would have known from her last look at me that she wanted me to like her. And I would have known that she was good and kind, too.

But I didn't know. There were a lot of things I didn't know. I sure learned.

Chapter Four: The First Blow is Struck

 On Saturday night Digger called Curtis and said he was coming right over to tell us something. He sounded upset and angry, and when he came over, we found out why. "Somebody busted into the clubhouse and took our table," he said. "And the right door is out of its runner, and the runner's been bent so badly I can't get the door back into it."

Nobody bothered to correct him on calling our rendezvous point a clubhouse. We all wanted to go see it, and Dad said he would go with us.

We trudged over a few streets to get to it. Everybody walked so fast that I could hardly keep up without breaking into a trot. Nobody had asked me how the day had gone with Miss Harris, and I was glad. I would have honestly said I didn't like her and thought she was lazy and just a little weird, and Mom and Dad would have lectured me on being critical. So it was just as well that nobody asked me.

We surveyed the shed by the light of our flashlights. It was just like Digger had described. Everything was gone, and one of the doors was out of its runner, so that it wouldn't close the right way.

"I think I can pound the runner back out straight," Dad said. "And re-fit the door to it. I'll do that Monday." He glanced up at us in the glare of our flashlights. "You kids have any idea who did this?"

"Sure, those three bullies," I said.

The other Sword Bearers and Shield Maidens glanced at me as though they'd forgotten or hadn't noticed that I'd come along, but Dad asked, "What three bullies are those?"

Rebecca told him, and Digger even told him Eddie's name. Dad sighed. Dad knew it was going to be pretty useless to call anybody's parents about the table and door. Eddy Reinbach had done things a lot worse than this and gotten off with no sweat.

And there was no evidence that Eddy and his pals had done this, but who else would have? The table wasn't worth anything. Somebody had taken it out of plain meanness.

"They didn't get Smaxcaliber, did they?" Rebecca asked.

"Of course not!" Digger exclaimed. "I'd never leave Smaxcaliber locked up anywhere. It sits in my bedroom when it's not with us at the meetings." Smaxcaliber meant a lot to all of us. It was almost as good as a real sword.

At last Dad stood up. "Well," he said. "Looks like you kids have a fight on your hands. We can fix the door and find another table, and I'll even padlock the place for you. But I think these kids really resent your being here."

"What should we do, Dad?" Curtis asked.

Dad shrugged. "We'll have to see what they do. But don't look for a fight."

Everybody nodded, and we started back to the house.

But Curtis whispered to me, "I got an idea. A Sword Bearer idea."

"What's that?" I asked.

"I'll tell you later. Come to my room, okay?"

Rebecca and Curtis were the partners of the family. Everybody knew that. I mean, they were twins. And even though only two years separated Curtis and me, it seemed like a lot more. He was big for his age, and I was small, and Curtis was Mr. Personality. He just seemed older and more sure of himself than any kid ought to be. With my big thick glasses and meekness, I seemed young.

But I came to his room while Rebecca worked away in our room on Spanish declensions of something or other.

"What's up?" I asked.

He threw his arm around my shoulders. "Jean, old pal, your brother Curtis's gonna' cut you in on a great adventure," he said.

"Why not Rebecca?" I asked him.

"Not Rebecca because this job requires only the brains and skill of one, and I can supply them."

"Thanks a lot."

"However, it does require the approximate dimensions of you," he added.

"What?" I asked.

"I'm trying to tell you that your older brother has figured out where our table is. But he needs you to help get it back."

"What will Dad say?"

"You heard him," Curtis reminded me. "He said he doesn't want us giving up. I say, we go rescue our table. What's the harm in that?"

"We might get our faces pushed into the dirt."

"No sweat, kid. There's no dirt for at least eighteen inches. Not with all that snow. And," he added. "I'll get that table when Eddy Reinbach is far away."

"Are you going to have him trailed?"

"No, silly. He's in the public high school. We get out of classes forty-five minutes before they do. And that yard bird probably has detentions every day for ninety years. Now look," he added. "This is your chance of a lifetime to come out like a hero. Are you with me?"

"Okay, sure," I said.

"Okay, sure," he mimicked. "We're from the Hall of Heroes! Say it right!"

I tried not to groan. "I pledge you my word on it," I told him.

"And not a word to the others. This must be our coup!"

"It can be our coup," I agreed. "What's a coup?"

He guided me to the door. "I'll let you know what day. Okay?"

"Okay?" I mimicked. "What kind of talk is that?"

"Brief and to the point. Remember, you promised to keep it between us."

"I'll keep my promise. But if he catches us, he'll hang us up by our Sword Bearer horns and use us for target practice. I pledge you my word on that, too."

Chapter Five: The Hall of Heroes Plans a Coup

 Curtis didn't want to make his move until Dad had gotten the shed door fixed and had a padlock for us, so we had to bide our time. Then on Thursday eighteen inches of snow fell from morning until night. Everybody got out of school early, and there was no school for anybody in the county on Friday.

That was always a good announcement for me, but Curtis was so disappointed that I think he would have really preferred going to school in all that snow and missing out on the sledding and snowball fights.

We convened a meeting of the Hall of Heroes, too. But we held it in Digger's kitchen in exchange for helping him clear out the drive way, the front walk, and the back walk and cleaning all the snow off his grandmother's car.

Smaxcaliber lay across the table amid our cups of hot chocolate. Suzette was with us, too, so the group was complete.

"How did your day as a Young Help go?" Suzette asked me. Obviously, this was one of Suzette's good days. Or maybe she was just behaving extra nicely because Digger's grandmother was watching us from the living room and cross-stitching in that nervous, exact way she has of jabbing the needle into the taut ring of cloth, in and out, as though cross stitching were just one more painful thing that had to be done.

I told them about Miss Harris.

"She does sound lazy," Curtis said.

"But she doesn't lock kids in her cellar," I retorted sharply.

"Not that we know of, " he shot back. "Not until she fattens 'em up."

"Seems like Mr. Orlando would only include people he approved of in the Young Helps program," Rebecca said doubtfully.

Digger shook his head. "I don't know. Maybe she said she needed a helper and he found her one. I mean, it's not up to him to decide how sincere people are when they ask for help is it? It's not like Mr. Orlando can go to their houses and grade them." And he laughed at the idea.

"She wants me back, so I'm going," I told them.

"You want someone to go with you?" Digger asked.

I shook my head. "I think she would know--you know--that I was doing it because I don't really like her. And it's not fair not to like her. I know that. She's just not what I pictured when I volunteered."

"Maybe you should just give her more time." Digger said.

Digger was right, of course. I kept telling myself that on the way over to the older part of town the next Saturday, and I kept telling it to myself as I counted mailboxes to the ninth house, and as I stood at the door and prepared for the long wait until she answered my knock.

But on this Saturday Miss Harris answered pretty quickly. She was in her robe and slippers, but she didn't retire to her bed this time.

"I'm so glad that you came," she told me. She took my coat for me. While I dusted the heavy furniture, she tidied up her room. The dining room table sat under its vast pile of papers the same as the week before, and I couldn't tell whether the papers had been moved at all or not.

The clutter of dishes in the sink wasn't quite so vast this week, and I got through them pretty quickly. Vacuuming came last. While I did this Miss Harris actually carried a load of laundry into the washing machine. The washer and dryer stood in a little corner in the kitchen, and I should have mentioned that both machines were covered with piles of laundry in various states of dirty, damp, dry, and folded.

After I had finished vacuuming, I put the cleaner away and went out to tell her that I was ready to leave. By then she was back in her place on the couch, and as I came in, she said, "I've made you some hot cocoa before you go, Jean. Here it is."

It was real cocoa, not the instant stuff. I sat down on the couch and took it from her, a pretty china cup on a saucer. "Thank you," I said.

"You work so hard. I'm really very grateful to you."

"Oh, that's fine." I looked around the room. By the stairway railings there was a whole gallery of framed photographs. They filled up the wall.

"Is that your family?" I asked her.

"The pictures to the left are of a Christian orphan home in Mexico," she told me. "The pictures to the right are of a home in Uganda, Africa."

"Do you know people there?" I asked.

"I served as a missionary to the home in Mexico for seven years," she told me. "I spent ten years in Africa--various parts. But the home in Uganda was very dear to me. Perhaps because I have no children."

"So you were a missionary," I said.

The news surprised me. I took a second look at her, and she smiled at me. "Yes, I've only been back in the states for nine months or so. Not long."

In the pictures she was lively, dressed up, as though she had always been busy and moving. Not like now. Seventeen years on the mission field. She had gone to the mission field before I had ever been born. So she had to be around forty years old, I figured. Maybe people slow down a lot when they're forty. Or maybe she hadn't been much good as a missionary. But in the pictures she looked like a good one. There were kids hanging all over her. She looked very young in all the pictures: laughing or shouting or smiling.

Maybe, I told myself, she came home to rest. So that's what she's doing all the time, resting. But if she rests too much, she'll never get going again.

I took my own cup back out to the kitchen, washed it, and set it in the drainer. I struggled into my coat as I walked back to the living room to say goodbye to her.

She helped me get buttoned up, and she wrapped my scarf for me, then took my hands like she'd done the week before. "I hope I'll see you next Saturday. I look forward to your visits."

By this time I felt pretty sure that the Lord wanted me to stick with it and not quit Young Helps. So I said, "Yes, I'll come back at the same time, okay?" I looked up at her, and she gave me that same kind of look, right into my eye if you know what I mean, deliberate, but gentle. I realized that--okay, maybe she was lazy--but she was kind. And she liked me. And she wanted me to like her. I would try. Maybe somebody who spent 17 years living in poor places was allowed to be lazy a while. I pulled on my gloves and went home through the snow.

There was school on Monday morning. As we trudged through the snow together, Curtis, Rebecca, and me, Curtis got over alongside me and whispered, "This afternoon we make our move. Go straight home after school and get into old clothes, then meet me at the corner."

"If you say so."

"Come on, Jean. We're the Hall of Heroes."

"I said I'd do it."

47

I guess I was kind of honored that Curtis would pick me to be his sidekick. I mean, probably out of all of the members of the Hall of Heroes, Curtis had the hardest time letting me in on things. Curtis likes to run things so much that sometimes he gets really impatient with me because I'm younger.

It was true that if I could help get the table back I would seem a lot more daring than I ever had before. But I had a wretched feeling that we were going to get caught.

That afternoon I did exactly as Curtis had ordered, but he was already at the corner waiting for me when I got there.

"It's about time," he said. "I was afraid you'd chickened out."

We started walking, with Curtis taking long strides that I hurried to keep up with.

"Okay, here's the plan," he said, talking in a low voice from the side of his mouth. "Eddy Reinbach's got this huge basement at his house. How do I know? Gus Frennel at church spent three months last year helping Eddy's dad finish the walls of the place. But they never got the job done. So they use the basement to store old junk."

"Are you sure Eddy put the table down there?" I asked.

"It's a cinch," he told me. "Where else could he put it where nobody would even notice it?"

"Sounds reasonable," I admitted.

"That's where you come in. I've taken a look at the place, and there's a narrow window I think I can boost you through. Then you can come around and let me in through the outside door and we'll get the table out."

"What if someone's in there and you boost me right through to them?" I asked.

"Don't worry. We'll listen first and make sure the place is empty."

Well, I was really scared, but I didn't want to say so to Curtis. I knew he'd get mad if I chickened out that far into the plan.

Normally we wouldn't have gone walking on the block where Eddy lived, but we knew that he and his thug friends would be in school for another thirty minutes. So we made a beeline to his back yard. The Reinbach house was a big split level. The front of it had the first floor level with the ground, but then the yard sloped downhill slightly, so that as you came around the back, the back wall of the basement was visible. A basement door opened onto the back yard.

Curtis pointed up to a high and narrow window that opened into the basement. "See," he said. "I think you can wiggle through that."

"I'm not sure, Curtis. And it's awful high," I told him. "You can't boost me that high."

Truthfully speaking, he wasn't going to admit that to me.

"Well, it is a little high," he conceded. "But if Rebecca were here, she wouldn't complain about it."

"Maybe you'd like to go back and get her," I said. "Because that would be fine with me."

"I didn't say anything about going and getting her!" he exclaimed. "Sheesh! Would you quit being so sensitive? I've got an idea."

"What?"

"There's a whole stack of firewood over there. I'll pile it up and stand on it to boost you through. You don't even have to help."

"I'd better help. Those guys will be getting out of school in twenty minutes."

I could also see that Curtis had completely forgotten that we had a time limit. He looked a little aggravated when I reminded him of it.

"No," he said. "Let me stack it up. I've got it all planned out in my mind."

"Okay, go ahead."

I knew he just wanted to do it himself because I always get in his way, and maybe because later he could brag to the others that it was his engineering alone that got us in. I started to realize that this was nothing like Curtis and Rebecca's partnership. They worked together when they did things, but Curtis was just bossing me around. He'd only wanted me because I was smallest and could fit through the window.

He went back and forth from window to woodpile, getting more and more logs.

"Better hurry," I told him. "Fifteen more minutes."

"Would you cool it?" he asked. "It'll be done in a minute."

I was afraid he might actually get me boosted through that window, and I started trying to imagine how in the world I would climb down the other side-- inside the basement. Then I would have to grope my way through that dark basement, trying to find the door. On this thought I reached over and touched the door. It had a pane of glass in it, so I figured that inside the dark basement I would be able to see some faint light coming through the window.

Then I would fumble around until I found the knob--and on this thought I reached down and took the knob--and then I would turn it and let Curtis in. As I thought about it, I turned it, and it yielded to me. I pushed the door to the basement open.

"Curtis," I said.

"Not now Jean. Quit nagging," he said. He had his parka pulled open, and his scarf hung open on either side of the hood. A pretty good sized pile of wood lay at his feet.

"But Curtis,"

"For crying out loud!" he exclaimed, and he spun around. He stopped when he saw the open door. "Oh," he said. He stepped up to the open doorway and looked at me. "Well come on," he said.

We only had eight minutes left, so I didn't stop to yell at him.

The basement was really big, and there was stuff everywhere. Curtis found the string to a dusty electric light bulb, and he pulled it on. I started to feel a little nervous about what we were doing--going into someone else's basement. I mean, I knew we were getting what was ours, but it seemed like the police-- not to mention our Dad--might take a different view on it.

And I was getting more and more convinced that Curtis had only brought me along to get the door opened for him. He'd flattered me and coaxed me and everything, but this was not a partnership at all. Except we would both equally share the blame when

Dad found out, and I was pretty sure that Curtis would be glad to unload half of that task onto me.

"There it is, Jean!" he exclaimed.

Sure enough, our splintery, rickety old table stood upright in a clear space in the basement.

"You get the back end, I'll get this end," he said, generously letting me take the end that would allow me to walk forward while he walked backward.

We brought it out of the basement, and just as Curtis got out the door, while I was still inside, I heard a yell.

"They've found us!" I exclaimed. "It's Eddy and his friends! We're caught!"

Trapped in Eddy's own basement! What could be worse?

"Let's go!" Curtis exclaimed. "Run for it!"

Chapter Six: The Basement Raid

 "We still have four minutes!" I exclaimed.

"Run!" Curt yelled. "Don't let go!"

I knew--after all we'd gone through--not to let go of the table. I pushed it into Curt, who was quickly changing hands so that he could run frontwards. We ran out the door and through the next yard over to get to the street. The tabletop was really small, so we were nearly running shoulder to shoulder as we went. It was so small that in some ways it was more awkward than a full sized table, but it was a lot lighter than a bigger table would have been.

"Where are they?" I yelled to him.

"Up on the back deck!" he yelled back. "They're comin' after us!" He looked back over his shoulder. "Faster, Jean! Faster! Here they come!"

We pelted through the snow to the street.

"Run to the rendezvous point!" he yelled. "I told the others to wait for us there!"

"They know about this?" I yelled.

"No, I said I had a surprise for them! Faster, Jean!"

Curt's a pretty fast runner, but I'm not. Anyway, I'm not very fast compared to three high school kids. And I knew that Curt--even if he were on his own--wouldn't be able to outrun them forever. What saved us was that Eddy and his friends were so mad that they started throwing snowballs and slush at us as we ran. The second that it took to scoop up snow each time they made a snowball helped us keep our lead.

Of course, snow and slush was hailing down around us like missiles on a battlefield, and we both got hit, but we didn't slow down. We got onto the street where the rendezvous point was, and Curt yelled, "Digger! Digger!"

"Help!" I yelled.

The three bullies quit throwing snowballs and worked on closing our lead before the other Heroes got to us. But they'd caught on to our plan too late. Digger popped out of the shed and came running. Suzette and Rebecca followed after him.

More snowballs rained after us, and I saw the girls stop to scoop up snowballs on their own. Digger didn't stop to do it, but he grabbed up snow as he ran, and he was good at throwing snowballs. He pitched them really hard at the three boys chasing us. "Get it into the clubhouse!" he yelled to us as we ran up to him.

"Rendezvous point!" I yelled as we went by.

We threw it into the clubhouse and went back to assist in the fighting.

Anyway, Curt went to assist. I could hardly breathe after that race through the snow. I made a show at making snowballs to throw, but I wasn't good for much. All I wanted was to catch my breath.

We weren't really needed, anyway. Eddy and his gang kept their distance and at last retreated, shouting at us as they went.

Curt said that the best way to tell Dad about what we did was just to tell him right out, so we did.

I was surprised at what an actor Curt was. He looked really sorry when he told Dad that we went into the Reinbach's basement to get our table back. I wasn't sorry. I didn't pretend that I was.

"We played the man, Dad," I told him as we sat around the dining room table after dinner. Mom abruptly got up and went into the kitchen.

"You played the man?" he asked me. "You did?"

"Curt did. I played the shield maiden."

Curt gave me a look to tell me to quit bragging about it. But Dad said, "Well tell me, are you brave enough, Miss Shield Maiden, to go to the Reinbachs and apologize for breaking and entering?"

Dad!" Curt exclaimed.

"Dad, they don't care," I told him. "They'd be just as glad that we came back and got our own table and didn't bother them about Eddy's taking it. You know that's true."

He did give me a look that showed that he knew it was true. But he said, "It's still not right to break into somebody's basement, Jean. And you know that."

"Can I tell you something else?" I asked him. "I don't want to talk back to you, but there's something else."

"All right, what is it?"

"The door to the basement was open. So it wasn't breaking and entering. We just walked in and got our table."

"It was our table," Curt said quietly. "And they stole it from us."

"I mean, Dad," I told him. "Didn't bigger kids ever pick on you? Didn't you ever have to do something yourself to stop them? Can't you see it from our point of view?"

He stopped and looked at me, and I kind of got the impression that he wanted to laugh about something. Mom came back in.

"I'm going to give you back your own words," he told me at last. "Yes, I can see it from your point of view. I do respect the spot that you're in. So this is the deal: from now on you bring these plans and ideas to me, when it comes to these three kids. I will see it from your point of view and will help you. You trust me, and I'll trust you. And I won't say anything else about this table adventure."

"Well that seems fair to me," I said. Mom left again.

Curt gave me a sharp glance and said, "Yes, Dad."

Chapter Seven: A Surprise at Martha Harris's

 The second time I'd gone to Miss Harris's I had kind of dreaded it. But by the third time I was more bored than anything else. It was just such a dull way to spend two hours.

But when I got there, I found that Miss Harris had company. In fact, a short, kind of tough looking woman met me in the doorway.

"Where's Miss Harris?" I asked her.

"Martha is sick today. She can't have visitors," the woman told me.

"I'm her cleaning girl."

She frowned and told me to wait there. I wondered why somebody as quiet and slow as Martha Harris would hang around with such a stern old lady. Because, this old lady had *bossy* vapors just steaming off of her.

In a few minutes the round woman came back and said, as she opened the door, "All right, she'll see you for a few minutes. But be quiet."

"Shouldn't I vacuum?" I asked her as I took off my own coat.

"No, you mustn't vacuum. Go back to her bedroom and say hello to her." She eyed my coat as though she thought it would be best for me to leave it on and go away as soon as possible. I didn't want to take up any more time, so I just hung it on the back of one of the dining room chairs instead of putting it in the closet.

I had come to clean, not visit, but this woman didn't seem to get the idea. I walked back through the hallway, through the living room, and into the back room that served as Miss Harris's bedroom.

Martha Harris lay propped up on pillows, dozing. She was even more pale than she had been during my last two visits. White, ghost-like, and very still. There was no doubt that she was sick. I took a couple steps into the room, and she turned her head to look at me as though it were a great effort to move. Her eyes had dark circles under them. I remembered that my mother would sometimes say that about one of us when we felt sick--"Oh my, you have dark circles under your eyes!" And I would always take a look for myself and could never see the dark circles. But today I could.

"Jean," she said, very quietly. "I should have called you. I don't think you should clean today."

"Do you have a stomach virus?" I asked. I kept my voice very quiet, because the closer I got to her, the more I could see that she felt terrible.

"No, dear. I'll be all right in another twelve hours or so."

I came up to her bedside and looked at her. The pupils of her eyes were very dilated, too.

"It was very good of you to come in to see me. I can hardly move, though, without getting sick." She let her hand, dry and hot, rest over mine. I felt really sorry for her, and I was glad, too, that she wasn't the kind of person who gets grumpy over being sick. She did look as though any motion would make her throw up. I was careful to gentle my voice as much as I could.

"I'll pray for you to start feeling better," I told her.

She smiled. "Thank you. You're a sweet girl."

"It's time you tried to get some sleep, Martha," the stern woman said, coming into the doorway. Her voice interrupted the quietness of the room. Miss Harris looked at her without moving her head.

"This was the last one," Martha said to her. "I can rest as much as I like from now on."

"It's now that you need it."

I wanted to ask her who the woman was, but I didn't dare, not with her standing there glaring at me.

"Will you come tomorrow, Jean?" Miss Harris asked me. "Just to visit me?"

"Sure," I told her. "After church."

"Yes. I doubt I'll be at church in the morning. I'll see you sometime in the afternoon, all right?"

I don't know how I had the nerve to do it, not being sure that I liked Miss Harris at all and having that stern, round woman hovering over me like a hawk about to snatch me away. And I wasn't perfectly sure that Martha Harris would like it, but before I thought about that, I leaned forward and carefully kissed her cheek. I was glad that it didn't make her throw up or anything. And she was glad that I did it. She smiled at me. Then the other woman hurried me away.

"You're a good girl," she said as she practically chased me up the hall to get my coat. "But Martha needs rest. If you come tomorrow, you behave as nicely as you did today, though I won't be there to watch you."

I wasn't sure about Martha Harris, but I was sure that I didn't like this woman, whoever she was. She wore a loose yellow sweater with many pulls in it, thrown over a plain white dress.

When I got home so early, my mother asked me what had happened, and I told her.

"Yes," she said. "I believe that somebody at church did tell me that Martha is sickly. Not many people there know much about her. Her family once lived in this area, but she's been away for years. She returned to the family house only a few months ago."

"She was a missionary," I said.

Mom nodded. "That's probably why Mr. Orlando had her join the Young Helps program. If she's recovering from an illness that she caught on the mission field, she probably still needs some help around the house. And I'm sure that she can be of help to you, too, once she's feeling better. It's good for you to see that missionaries are just regular people."

Mom and Dad had both told us before not to think that pastors and missionaries were perfect people or super people who had some kind of "in" with God. So I knew that it was a good thing to help Miss Harris and get to know her. And by the end of that day I decided that, yes, I did like her after all. She was different from most people, but she was nice, and she didn't complain about being bossed around by that stern lady, whoever *she* was.

"The older woman sounds like a nurse," my mom told me. "Are you sure that white dress of hers wasn't a nurse's uniform?"

"Why would a nurse be at Miss Harris's house?" I asked.

"There is such a thing as home health care, Jean," Mom told me. "Some nurses make rounds to the houses of their patients."

"Well maybe she is a nurse," I told her. "Are all nurses that bossy?"

Mom laughed. "You know Mrs. Crawford from church. Is she bossy?"

"No," I admitted.

"It just depends on the person. I've got some soup in the freezer. I'll thaw it in the microwave tomorrow and send it over with you. That will help Martha out a little, I'm sure."

So the next day, after church and after dinner, I took the jar of chicken soup in a heavy brown bag and trudged back over to Martha Harris's house.

There was a note on the door knob. It said, JEAN. I opened it and read, COME INSIDE. I'M IN THE BACK. MARTHA

I poked my head inside and looked around. No sign of the nurse. All was clear. The soup I put into the refrigerator. I took off my coat and then hung it up properly, and at last I went back to Martha Harris's room.

She did look a lot better today. Some color had come back to her face, and the area around her eyes was almost back to normal.

She had her Bible on her lap and a book called TREASURY OF DAVID alongside her. At sight of me she smiled and held out her arms. I didn't even think about it. I just went and gave her a hug.

"My mom sent some soup for you," I told her. "Should I get you some?"

"Not just yet. I'm ready to enjoy our visit, and I don't even want to interrupt it with eating."

"Was that woman who was here yesterday a nurse?" I asked her.

"Mrs. Everett," she replied. "Yes, she's a nurse. She comes to see me when I'm feeling poorly."

"Are you sick a lot?" I asked. It might not have been polite to ask that, but I forgot. I really wanted to know.

"I won't be as much anymore," she told me. "Not for a long time. You could start coming more often if you like." She put her hand under my chin and looked at me with a smile. "I'm so happy that the Lord sent you to me. I'll be able to spend more time with you if you like."

"Will we start cleaning the upstairs?" I asked.

She laughed her slow and relaxed laugh. "We don't have to clean all the time."

That was her laziness speaking, I thought. But it wouldn't have been nice to argue or contradict.

"You have to tell me about yourself," she said. "That's more important than cleaning. About yourself, about your family if you want, about what the Lord has done for you and what you think about Him."

Her request took me by surprise. "Why?" I asked.

"I thought we might be friends."

That made sense. In a way we already were friends. "Well okay," I told her. "I kind of got in trouble yesterday over rescuing a table. Can I tell you about that?"

Her eyes became very curious in their slow, quiet way, and she said, "Was the table in great danger?"

"Not as much as I got into," I told her. "But I still pulled it off. With my brother."

"Yes, I would like to hear this," she said, and nodded.

Chapter Eight: Superior Brains, Superior Courage, And Superior Skill

 We had a padlock on the shed now, so we knew that the table was safe. Every time we finished up a meeting, Digger would make a big show of padlocking the metal shed and would then hand the key to Curt to keep.

We all felt pretty smug about getting the table back, and since we had seen Eddy and his pals run away every time all five of us showed up together, we never bothered to post a watch during our meetings.

When ever we would rally at the rendezvous point, we kept the door open because it was so dark and so cold in the rendezvous point. We just let the padlock hang on the door latch, on the outside. After each meeting, Curt and Digger would push and pull on the door to slide it closed. Then Digger would put the latch over a metal ring on the door frame, thread the padlock through the ring, and lock it closed.

Rebecca brought a thermos jug of hot chocolate to our next meeting, and we had it and congratulated each other on our victory over Eddy and his friends.

"Friends, there's nothing like superior brains, superior courage, and superior skill," Digger said to us.

"Not to mention superior numbers," Rebecca added. Suzette laughed.

We had a pretty good time all around, making fun of Eddy and his friends, which I know was not very charitable of us. Digger said that when brains were being passed out, Eddy thought they said trains, so he ordered one that was made of iron. We all laughed at that. I know it wasn't right, but we got our payback pretty quickly.

We'd been going for about ten minutes, making fun of them and having a good time, when all of a sudden the door to the shed snapped closed.

"Hey!" Digger exclaimed. It was dim but not perfectly dark in there, because the door wasn't well sealed. Light came in through the cracks around it. We heard the padlock click into place.

"Hey! We're in here!" Rebecca yelled.

"It's Eddy and his friends!" Curt told her.

"They've locked us in!" Digger exclaimed.

My heart thrilled with fear at the first thought of being locked in that cold shed. But it only took me a second to calm down. We could probably break out, and if we couldn't, Mom and Dad knew where we were and would come get us by dark. Digger and Curt pulled on the door and shook it in its frame. "We can bend it out if we have to--" Curt began. But just then the whole floor lurched. The thermos clattered to the floor, and I fell into Rebecca. Suzette screamed.

"Hey!" Digger yelled.

"They're tipping us over!" Suzette screamed.

"Hang on, girls!" Curt yelled.

"To what?" Rebecca asked. She grabbed the table and pushed it against the back wall. The floor heaved up again and almost--it seemed to me-- separated from the walls. These metal outdoor sheds aren't built to stand a lot of shifting. Not with the weight of five people in them.

I realized then how Eddy and his friends were tipping us. They were wedging stuff up under one end of the skids under the floor, pushing us further and further back.

Digger lost his temper and really started yelling at them. He told them to come in and fight like men and not cowards. But that was impossible. They couldn't come in if they'd wanted to, because they didn't have a key to the padlock.

The floor tipped up more and more, and we all crowded back to the lower side, since that was the way the shed would fall. Outside, Eddy yelled "Chop!"

And then his two friends joined in, and they all yelled "Chop!"

We tipped more precariously. Digger pulled my hood up over my head.

"Chop!" they shouted. And then finally, "T-i-i-mber!" And the shed fell over with us inside.

Even though we'd been tipped pretty far over, it was still quite a jolt to fall the rest of the way. There was a crash when the shed toppled over, and for a minute everyone was kind of stunned.

At last Curt spoke: "Is everyone all right?"

Suzette sat up. "The floor's bent out of the wall," she said.

Rebecca sat up, too. She looked at the floor--which was now facing us. "Yeah," she agreed.

It was dim in the shed, but even less dim than it had been, because some of the joins between the floor and the walls had opened. Digger stood up, stooped over. He picked up Smaxcaliber. The shed doors were now over our head. They weren't difficult for Digger to explore with his hands.

"Now how do we do this?" he asked.

"Use Smaxcaliber to pry open the doors as far as the latch will allow," Curt said. "Have Jean try to slip her hand through and unlock the padlock."

I shook my head. "The door won't open that far right near the latch," I told him. "And even if I could get the key through and do it, I'd never get the padlock off the latch."

Digger agreed with me. "Here's the place where your Dad pounded that runner out straight again," he said. "Let's pry it open and force the bottom door of the door inward."

He and Curt took out their pen knives and worked on prying the runner flat. Curtis' knife broke, and so Digger worked alone. It was getting colder by the minute inside that shed. We were all shivering. Finally, he managed to pry the runner open far enough to use the ax handle. Digger pushed Smaxcaliber through the tiny slit of space between the bottom of the door and the wooden flooring. He pried the door back. It gave easily and allowed a big enough hole for me to squeeze through. I climbed out and clambered to the ground then came around the side of the toppled shed and unlocked the padlock. I opened the latch. The others pushed and pulled the door open wide enough and came out, first the girls, and then Curt and Digger. They climbed off the wreck and surveyed what had been our rendezvous point.

"Dad'll love this story," I told Curt. We stood in a dismal group for a long moment.

"Let's get it back up," Digger ordered. He looked mad.

It took a long time to get the shed righted. It was hard to grip, and we had been chilled so badly while inside it that we were more tired than we had expected. And the shed itself moved and wobbled on the flooring. It seemed that we would pull it apart if we didn't move it upright as a unit.

After about ten minutes Suzette said she had to go home now, and she left. Rebecca looked like she really wanted to go, too. But she didn't. For the first time I saw Digger get irritated, and then mad.

"Look Curt, if you'd like to do this your own way, why not just do it yourself?" he demanded of Curt as the shed fell back for about the fourth time.

"What are you talking about?" Curt asked.

"When I say to push, you just stand there."

"I am pushing!" Curt exclaimed.

"Could we fight about this later?" Rebecca snapped. "Who came up with this stupid clubhouse idea, anyway?"

"You did!" Curtis yelled. "You and Suzette! Suzette the Deserter!"

I kept my mouth shut. It was no time for the youngest to come up with any ideas.

"Stop fighting and start pushing!" Digger shouted.

At last, after about six tries we got it back up, but it sat kind of funny because the floor wasn't joined to the walls right anymore.

Digger went home his way, and we went home our way. It wasn't like the Hall of Heroes had split or anything, but everybody was out of sorts. And Curtis was really mad at Suzette. I was glad about that.

When we told Mom and Dad the story, they were really flummoxed by it. Dad just kind of stared at us for a minute. Then he got his hat and coat, and we all went to take a look at the rendezvous point.

We all wanted to call the police, but Dad said it wouldn't do much good. For one thing, none of us had seen who locked us in. So there was no way to prove that Eddy and his pals had done this.

Most of the Hall of Heroes was pretty mad about what had happened, and Dad was annoyed at having to fix the shed again. But I couldn't help but see the funny side of it. Maybe being the youngest and least noticed of the group had made me a little hard hearted to the older ones. Or maybe I was just being objective. I mean, we really had been smug, and we'd been in the very act of making fun of Eddy and his friends when they'd ambushed us.

That night after we'd all talked about what to do without coming up with any answers, I saluted Curt with my cup as we brushed our teeth. "Here's to superior brains, superior courage, and superior skill," I said. He did not think that was funny.

Chapter Nine: More About Martha Harris

 On Saturday I told Miss Harris about our latest adventure at the rendezvous point. Telling her that story involved telling her about the Hall of Heroes and the Sword Bearers and Shield Maidens.

"My," she said when I'd finished. "What an interesting life you've had."

"My life's not interesting," I told her. "Except when I can't help it and get sucked into one of Curt and Rebecca's adventures."

"But you're a part of the Hall of Heroes."

"I think that the Lord did that to me," I told her. "Because I'm a coward. He's trying to make me brave."

We were sitting out on her sofa. Miss Harris was feeling a lot better that day. She made cocoa for me and hot mint tea for herself, and a needlepoint hoop sat alongside her. She'd obviously been working on it.

It was a sampler for a baby. I meant to tell her that I was glad she was over her flu or virus or whatever it had been, but before I said it, she asked, "Jean, what made you think that the Lord wanted you to get more courage?"

"Well, because I am such a chicken, and Christians are supposed to be brave," I told her. "You think so, don't you?" I asked her that because it did occur to me that somebody who didn't mind being lazy might not mind being afraid, either.

"I think that saying Christians are supposed to be brave is a little like saying that babies are supposed to walk. It's a true statement, but if you say it too soon or with too much rigor, you're being unreasonable." She reached over and gave a playful tug on my bangs; her eyes met mine with a kind of challenging look. "What is the chief purpose of man? Do you know?"

I recognized the question. It was one that we'd had to know in Bible class when I was younger.

"To know God and enjoy Him forever," I answered, correctly.

"Hmm, not to be brave," she remarked. I looked up at her again. "When we see God's face, we forget fear," she said. "Don't you know that perfect love casts out all fear?"

"But we won't see God's face until we go to heaven," I told her.

"We get close to seeing His face here on earth. And we can enter His presence while we're here on earth. Alone. Just the Christian and the Lord. That's enough to drive away fear. But the first thing is to love being in His presence." She looked at me and smiled, and I noticed how Miss Harris's hair, which was kind of blond and brown, parted exactly in the middle and fell away in exactly the same waves on each side. She was kind of pretty.

"I try to love God," I told her.

"I know, Dear. And even more, I know that you do love God. Do you know what else?"

"What?" I asked.

"He loves you. I am perfectly sure of that."

"He loves everybody," I told her.

She smiled at me again. "But He especially loves you. That's how I know that He'll bring you through your fears as the victor. And He'll show you the things you want to know about Him."

"How do you know all that?"

"I pray for you, Dear. The Lord has given me peace about those things." I realized that Miss Harris had been watching and thinking about me a lot more than I'd bothered to think about her.

Suddenly I felt the way I've felt when I've walked into a room where people have just been talking about me. It happened once or twice with Mom and Dad. I knew that whatever they were saying wasn't bad, but it felt strange to know that they'd been talking about me without me being there. And now I felt that way again.

I couldn't think of any small talk to say, but she said, after a moment, "The best way to know how God loves you is to simply ask Him to show you, Jean."

"Okay," I said.

She changed the subject and showed me the sampler and how far she had stitched on it and what it would look like. After that we talked about the pictures on the wall, and I asked her if the papers on the dining room table were letters that she was writing to all the children she'd known in Mexico and Uganda. She told me that her personal mail she usually wrote by hand.

"No," she added. "The work on the dining room table is much more serious than anything I would have to write. It's a translation of the Gospel of John into a trade language."

"Who are you typing it for?" I asked.

She sighed and then smiled at me, as though I'd said something funny.

"Dear Jean, I'm the translator."

"You are?" I asked. "Can you speak another language?"

Her smile broadened, but her eyes became more gentle. "I hide it well, dear, but I'm a philologist."

"A what?"

"I am a language expert. It was my job to get to know some of the various trade languages spoken throughout certain regions of Africa, select those that had a suitable written form, and translate parts of the Bible into them."

"I thought you worked in an orphanage."

"No. I took my rests there and stopped in as often as I might. The home was part of a larger compound. It was rather like a hub for many of us who were out in the field a lot." She must have thought that I was embarrassed at not knowing all this, but I didn't mind. I was too surprised. And to think, I had thought she was lazy.

She put her hand on my shoulder and pointed to the far wall, to a plaque that hung over by the bedroom doorway. "There is my sheepskin," she said.

"Sheepskin?" I asked.

"My degree. I have a Ph.D. in Field Linguistics."

I went over to the framed document on the wall. I had passed it often and never really noticed what it said. But when I read the ornate letters, I saw that she really had earned a Ph.D. And the degree had been awarded to Venus Martha Harris. I turned to her. "Is your name really Venus?"

She smiled as though I had discovered her guilty secret. "I come from a Southern family, and I'm afraid my people were always quite attached to old family names. Yes, dear, my first name is Venus. It was my grandmother's name as well, and her mother's name. It goes back for generations in my family. But to make life bearable, I've always gone by Martha."

I really took a second look at her that time. "You're really a doctor?" I exclaimed.

She smiled and gave a slight bow, but she swept out her hand as though making a flourish with it. "At your service. Dr. Martha Harris." Then she laughed, I suppose because I was so amazed. "It's nothing, Jean dear. You didn't know because I don't refer to it much."

I returned to the sofa. "But why not?" I asked.

"Because the chief end of man is to know God and enjoy Him forever. Degrees and accomplishments are nice enough, and I've used mine and enjoyed the learning process. But in the end, degrees are nothing, human accomplishment is nothing. Only God matters. And all that God cares about is a broken and a contrite heart."

And as she said that, some of her lightness disappeared, and her eyes got wet for a moment. But she smiled again. "There, that's my story."

"Did God want you to go to college?" I asked.

"He did, indeed. I got through college and grad school by relying on Him for money and strength and understanding. He gave me enough of all three. The important thing is to remember that He gave those things." As she said that, it hit me that I'd been all wrong about Martha Harris. I'd thought she was lazy and careless, but she wasn't.

"You're a godly woman," I said without thinking. I don't think it was bad to say it, but there was some surprise in my voice. But she didn't seem to notice the surprise.

"God loves me," she told me. "It's all that matters. And remember," she added, as she suddenly left the needle in the fabric and put her arms around me. "Enjoying a person involves nothing other than enjoying them." She looked at me with her deliberate look before she kissed my cheek and let me go.

The time had flown by. It was already eight thirty, and I had to go home. I wondered what she meant by enjoying a person means nothing other than enjoying a person.

I thought about it on the way home, and I thought about it while I took my bath that night, and I thought about it while I was in bed. I can see that Miss Harris enjoys me, I told the Lord. Because she talks to me, for one, but also because she does things for me, like the home made cocoa. And she hugs and kisses me. And she always looks me right in the eye before I leave. Except for the talking part, how does a person do all of that with You? How does a person know God and enjoy Him forever? How, Lord?

Then I remembered what Miss Harris had said about asking God to show me that He loved me. So I asked Him. If I was special to God like Miss Harris said I was special to God, I wanted to know it.

Chapter 10: The Hall of Heroes Takes Another Hit

 I had things on my mind I hadn't thought much about before. I had learned in school that it was important to have daily devotions and to spend time with the Lord. But Miss Harris had made it sound so much more--well, inviting.

I asked my mom about it.

"Jean," she told me. "A person might do all the right things, might be a genuine Christian, might even willingly sacrifice money and time for the Lord's work, and still miss the main point of Christianity."

"Well what is the main point of Christianity?" I asked her.

"To know God."

"I thought that meant being saved."

"Honey, it means being saved like being a part of a family means being born into it. Being saved is the foundation of it, and it's the starting point. But it's not the sum total of knowing God."

"Well that's just it," I told her. "When a person's a baby, everybody else does everything. I mean, the mother picks up the baby and takes care of it, and the baby can see its mother face to face, and you know, talk to her and kiss her and run to her. That's what makes a baby know it's a member of a family."

She nodded. I thought maybe she wouldn't have an answer, but she said, "God reaches out to us, Jean. Especially us, because we already belong to Him. And we know that He has a special love for children." She looked thoughtful and then added, "God does carry us, honey, more than we stop to think about it. He helps us along even when we aren't thinking about Him. And He showers us with loving gifts, just like good parents do for their children, but Christians can be very ignorant of His kindnesses. And yet, God is still very kind."

"So where do I start, then, if I want to know God--know Him a lot, I mean?" I asked.

"You start by asking Him to teach you. The Holy Spirit is our teacher and our Comforter. And He will teach you. I can tell you this much, sweetheart, you have to spend time with God in prayer, and when I say prayer I mean more than bringing petitions to God. I mean worshipping God."

I didn't want to talk about it anymore because I wasn't sure if I understood or not.

I'd already won a lot of Christian citizenship awards in school, and I was one of the "good kids" who always got to run messages down to the office or give my testimony in chapel. It almost seemed as though all of that didn't count for much. Mom had said so. A person could follow all the rules and go to church and still miss out. Knowing God got in the way.

I pushed it out of my mind for a while. It had been several days since our last adventure in the rendezvous point, and Dad had repaired it as much as he could. He didn't want us using it anymore. But we hadn't liked that decision.

"Mr. Anderson, it's like giving in to them," Digger pointed out to him that night after they'd finished the last of the repair work.

"I know that, Digger," Dad said. We were all around the dining room table, having cake. Smaxcaliber leaned against the wall. "I hate to have you give in to them, believe me. But you could get hurt. Those kids play rough."

"We could fight back," Digger told him. "Defend what's ours."

Dad nodded. "I wouldn't even mind that," he said. "There's a time and a place for defending yourself. The problem is that we cant be sure that they did it. I called the Reinbachs last night, and Eddy and his friends say they were skating after school last Monday. So there you are. They have other kids ready to vouch for them."

"We could post a watch at the rendezvous point," Digger told him. "Then if they come back for more trouble, we'll be ready."

"I don't know," Dad said.

"We can't let them just win, Dad," Curt pointed out.

Suzette wasn't there that night, but Rebecca spoke up for both of them. "We won't mind the danger," she said.

Dad rolled his eyes. "I know you won't mind the danger. That's the danger."

"How about if we take it on a meeting by meeting business?" Digger suggested. "We'll let you know every time we use it. That way if you want to stop by, it'll be fine. And we'll keep a watch. Maybe we can spot one of those kids and prove that they locked us in."

Dad at last agreed to the meeting-by-meeting plan. We let him know that we wanted to have another meeting the next day, and he okayed it.

We all felt better about our troubles, and I was pretty sure that Eddy and his friends were probably tired of hounding us anyway. They would probably leave us alone, now that they'd won such a major victory. And it was a major victory. There was no doubt on either side that the main course being served in the Hall of Heroes was humble pie.

However, I was wrong about them being tired of hounding us. They were really just getting warmed up.

The next afternoon I hurried out to the rendezvous point. As usual, I was the last one. I just couldn't get dressed and get something to eat as fast as Rebecca or Curt.

But when I got out to the lot, I saw Digger, Rebecca, and Curt all standing outside. I can't say that they were standing out side the clubhouse, because there was no clubhouse. There was nothing but the empty lot.

Chapter 11: The Hall of Heroes is Restless

"How do three kids move a whole shed?" I asked.

"They couldn't have done this," Curt said. "Somebody else did it. Those three couldn't have done it."

Digger shook his head. "Yes they could. It must have taken them all night, though. Look, there's tracks. They broke free the skids and dragged it away."

"All that work!" Rebecca exclaimed. "Moving the skids and pulling that whole shed! Was it really worth it to them?"

"I'm sure they were laughing the whole way," I said. "It must've given them a real charge to think of how stupid we'd look when we came out here and found our rendezvous point missing." Come to think of it, we really did look pretty stupid. But I didn't say that. All the same, my honest comment irritated Curt.

"Jean, nobody asked you," he said.

"Since when does Jean have to wait to be asked?" Digger demanded. "She's as much a part of the Hall of Heroes as you are."

"Would everybody please stop bickering?" Rebecca asked. "We've got to go tell Dad."

She was right, and we did slowly walk away from the site of our late clubhouse. But Digger kicked at the snow. "Go tell Dad! he exclaimed. "I'd like to go drag Eddy Reinbach away from his friends and--"

"Yeah, well you can't," Rebecca told him. "And don't stoop to it, okay? Those guys are just waiting for us. They know we're really mad. We'll think of something. Something better."

Everybody was grumbly and out of sorts. Dad called the police about the stolen shed, and he told Lt. McKenna all about our run-ins with Eddy and his pals. But Lt. McKenna looked doubtful. Knowing who had done it was one thing. Finding the shed and proving it were altogether different.

I felt really bad for the rest of the Sword Bearers and Shield Maidens of the Hall of Heroes. But then, I've always been the youngest, and so I've always been the one doing things wrong or getting taken by surprise. That night after dinner I climbed up into our attic where it was lonely and chill. I turned on the light bulb and sat on a crate of old books. And in my mind I slowly replayed the scene of everybody standing in the middle of the lot staring at the place where the clubhouse had been.

I laughed until I cried.

Miss Harris met me at the door Saturday completely dressed, with makeup on. She smiled at my surprise.

"Yes, I do have other clothes than just my robe," she said. "Come inside."

She had also done all of the dishes. The dining room table, though still under piles of papers and books, had obviously been tidied up as much as possible.

I dusted and vacuumed while she worked in the kitchen. As I put the vacuum cleaner away, she said, "Would you like to see the upstairs today?"

I'd been wondering what kind of mystery surrounded the upstairs of the Harris house. After all of my surprises Thursday night, Id come to think that anything might be upstairs, from a built-in pool to a trampoline.

But when we got upstairs I found only a single master bedroom, a bathroom, and another room made up as a kind of library and office. The bedroom was pretty, all done in blues. And the office was clean with lots of space on the desk for books.

"Miss Harris, why don't you use these rooms?" I asked. "This bedroom is so much nicer than the one downstairs."

"This is my real bedroom," she told me. "But I've been ill lately. It became too tiresome to walk up and down the stairs."

I hadn't realized that there had been more illness than the few days I had seen of it. Suddenly it all made sense. The house had been so badly kept because she'd been sick for a while. You're better now, right?" I asked her.

"I feel much better these days than I did, say, a month ago at this time," she told me. "Much better."

She put her arm around me. "We'll just have to see about tomorrow and the days after."

"I'm glad you're better," I told her.

"Why not come downstairs and help me make cookies," she suggested. "I don't think that the people I plan to send them to will miss a couple. Which do you like better, the cookies or the dough?"

"The dough," I told her.

"One of the best parts about being grown up is that you can eat as much of the dough as you like, and nobody tells you not to." With that, and a laugh, she led me downstairs.

We had a good time that day. In fact, I didn't get home until five o'clock. Just in time for supper.

"We had a Hall of Heroes meeting," Curt told me as I came through the door.

"I'm sorry I missed it. Nobody told me."

"Digger hung Smaxcaliber in the window, but you never came close enough to see it."

"Mom knew where I was," I told him. "Over at Martha Harris's house. We made cookies. And you know what, she can read Greek, Curt. She showed me. She has a Greek New Testament, and she showed me John 3:16 in it. It doesn't even look like English. How did those guys ever figure it all out?"

"What guys?" he asked.

"You know, Erasmus and Martin Luther and those guys."

"Who are you talking about?" he demanded.

"The preachers who said every man ought to have the Bible in his own language. She told me all about them. I thought you knew."

"You missed an important meeting," he told me.

"What happened?"

"Well." He held out his hands. "Nothing happened. But it was a the Hall of Heroes meeting."

"I couldn't help it," I said, and I admitted, "I don't even mind. I had so much fun with Miss Harris. You know, I never noticed it before, but she's beautiful. She is, Curt."

He got impatient. "You don't even care about the Hall of Heroes, Jean. Maybe you aren't part of it."

I got mad. "Hah!" I yelled. "Maybe I didn't go with you on that stupid adventure to steal back our table. And maybe I didn't get locked up in the shed with the rest of you and get slammed around. Hah!" I yelled again. "You just try to tell me I'm not a part of the Hall of Heroes, Curt!"

I walked about three steps away from him and spun back around. "I am a member of the Hall of Heroes, and I am a member of Young Helps, and never the twain shall meet!" Whatever that meant. I stomped away.

Curt didn't stay mad at me. The few times I've ever put my foot down I usually surprise everybody so much that no one argues with me. Over dinner, Mom asked me what we'd done that day, and I told her about it. Rebecca and Curt looked as though the idea of hanging around with a missionary lady all day was about as much fun as playing with a bag of hammers. But they didn't know Martha Harris.

It was hard to run over and see her during the week because of school and homework. But she was able to come out to church on Wednesday nights. Saturdays I spent the afternoon with her. She could do needlepoint and cross stitch, and she showed me how. I told her about the Hall of Heroes and about how our rendezvous point got stolen right from under our noses. And I told her about Eddy and his gang. I'd never even told my mom all the things I told Miss Harris, not all at once, anyway. Sometimes after a day with her I would wonder if I talked too much. But as it turned out, it was a good thing I did tell her all about Eddy and his gang.

Chapter 12: An Unexpected Rescue

 About a month went by. February hit like a block of ice, and it looked like it might go out that way, too. We still had plenty of snow everywhere. A warm day would come with lots of sunshine, and everybody's hopes would climb. But then it would snow for a whole night, and the whole town looked like it had looked in January.

In four weeks we were no closer to finding our clubhouse (or rendezvous point. Nobody had enough spirit to stick to details any more.) But we had plenty of troubles. Eddy and his friends must have made some pretty good notes on our schedules, because two or more of them kept turning up whenever one of us was left alone. I couldn't walk from our house down to the US mail box without getting showered with snowballs. Digger actually got into a fight with Eddy and Eddy's pal, Johnny. They jumped him. He did pretty well, too, for being by himself. You couldn't say he beat them up or anything, but then they couldn't beat him up either. He was so mad at them by this time that he just kept fighting no matter what. Finally, all three of them were so tired that they just kind of walked away from each other.

Dad was kind of angry himself. He'd called Eddy's parents a couple times, and he even talked to Lt. McKenna of the town Police force about it. But nothing did much good.

I didn't think that the Hall of Heroes had shaped up to being much of a heroic band. Suzette hadn't been showing up much at our meetings lately. It's not that she and Rebecca had both been doing other things together. Rebecca had no idea what was keeping Suzette so busy, except for volleyball practice. Suzette had made the team.

As for me, I liked being with Miss Harris more than I liked being in the Hall of Heroes. Not all the time, but a lot of the time.

The one time during the week that I had always been safe from Eddy and his friends was Saturday mornings when I would walk over to Miss Harris's. I had given up waiting until one o'clock to go over there. Now I went over at ten and did my housework.

From about eight until ten thirty or eleven, Miss Harris stayed in her room with the door only partly open. She spent that time "with the Lord," reading her Bible and praying. It seemed like a long time, to me. I didn't disturb her until she came out herself.

She usually made me lunch, though she never ate much herself. After lunch, we would visit and work on our cross stitch patterns, or I would help her organize the papers she had written while in Africa. She was trying to get them assembled for a textbook that a mission board wanted to publish for other people who would be training in field linguistics.

So one Saturday in early February, I wasn't really worried much about Eddy and his friends as I walked over to the older part of town. The hedges had snow on them, and there were deep ruts of snow and slush in the street. I had to kind of pick my way along. The snowplows had been busy lately, and these back streets hadn't been done in a while.

All of a sudden, blam, a really hard snowball hit me in the face. I nearly fell down, and I pulled off my glasses and swiped my sleeve across my eyes before I turned to run. But I ran right into somebody, who pushed me back. I pulled my glasses back on and found myself face to face with one of Eddy's goons. Eddy and the other one came out from one of the hedges.

"It's Jean Anderson," Eddy said. "She's out early today."

"Looks to me like she needs her face washed," the other one, Johnny, said.

"That's an idea," the one by me said. "There's some water right there," and he pointed to a puddle of slush in one of the ruts.

I knew they'd do it to me, and I got scared at the thought of them putting my face into that and holding me there. I did something that surprised even me. I didn't punch. I scratched. Just as he leaned close to say something else, I let him have it right across his face.

And then I ran.

I heard him yell in surprise, and Eddy and Johnny yelled, "Get her!" I fell right into one of the ruts and got up and kept running.

Like I said, I knew I could never outrace three high school kids. I wiggled through one of the hedges, getting snow all down my collar and into my scarf. It was a good high hedge, and it slowed them down while I sprinted for the next hedge.

This hedge strategy might have worked if it had been a matter of only two or three hedges between me and home base. But after four, I was so tired I couldn't wiggle through as fast as they could. They started to catch up to me.

Martha Harris's house was in plain sight, just up the street. I tried to race them on the straightaway, hoping I was far enough ahead. I got past the fifth house, sixth house, seventh house, but by the time I reached the driveway of the eighth house, they were so close they were snatching at me.

"Miss Harris!" I yelled. "Miss Harris. Help! Help!"

But I thought it was probably useless to yell. Martha Harris was not only a slow moving person, she was also heedless of what was going on sometimes. Especially when she was reading or praying. She prayed out loud, for one thing, quietly but in a regular voice, not a whisper. I doubted that she'd notice some kid yelling out in the street.

But I kept yelling, even at the last minute when I veered sideways through the long yard of the ninth house, her house, and tried to get to her back door, which would bring me to her kitchen.

They tackled me in the side yard and pulled me up. The one who I had scratched really was mad. He wasn't laughing any more about putting my face in the slush. He pulled his arm back and hit me across the face harder than I'd ever been hit. It cut short my yell for help.

"Hey!" It even surprised Eddy. "She's a kid."

"She's a brat! Look what she did!" he yelled back. There was a line of blood on his face where I'd scratched him with the fast, accurate scratch of a cat. Nobody had been more surprised by that than me.

Eddy pulled me away, not gently, either. "You paid her back then. Let's go find that wash basin."

I was really stunned from getting hit so hard, so I couldn't struggle or fight back, but just then Eddy gave a tremendous yell, and he dropped me. Then the boy who'd hit me yelled. Johnny leaped back, and a gush of water hit me on top of my head. I backed up.

Up above at the upstairs window, Martha Harris calmly leaned away from the open window and reappeared with a big tub. She upended it so fast that I leaped back close to the wall. But Eddy--who didn't see her until a second after I did--got most of it, even though he tried to dodge it.

Let me remind you that it was about thirty three degrees out there.

"Last chance before the police, Eddy Reinbach," Martha called down to them. "Go home and leave her alone."

"Let's go," Eddy said to his friends. He pointed at me "Stay off the streets!" And he whirled around with his friends and strode away.

Chapter 13: The Secret Fellowship

 My hair was hit by one of the splashes of water, and my slacks were wet from falling in the slushy street. Miss Harris wasted no time. She met me at the side door and pulled me inside. She was panting, but though she was out of breath, she directed me to get out of my things. She'd brought down spare clothes for me. These were clothes that were about my size--secondhand. She collected and mended clothing to send to one of the children's homes.

"Change into these," she gasped. Her cheeks were flushed. "I'll put your things into the dryer. There's a blow dryer in the bathroom upstairs."

I hurried into the borrowed clothes and went upstairs. By the time I had blow dried my hair, I could almost laugh about what had happened. Miss Harris was good enough to be a member of the Hall of Heroes herself.

113

It wasn't until I finished in the bathroom and came downstairs to see how my wet clothes were doing that I realized that Miss Harris was back in her robe again. She hadn't worn it on a Saturday in over a month. And she was still out of breath, but no longer panting. She didn't get up from the couch when I came downstairs, so I went over to her. The flush was gone from her cheeks, and she was pale.

But before I could say anything she said, "This is where that boy hit you, isn't it?" And she touched the raised welt on my cheek. "Are you all right?"

It made me wince, but I nodded. She looked at the welt and said, "I think it will be all right," but she stroked my cheek and hugged me. Then she looked into my eyes to make sure that my feelings weren't hurt from being hit. She seemed much more shaken up than I felt, so I said, "How'd you know which one was Eddy?"

"Oh I didn't," she admitted with an unsteady smile. She was still breathing with a slight wheeze. "I called down to all three of them, but Eddy looked up at his name. I'm glad that he was frightened off."

"Me, too! Maybe I should ask Digger if you can sign up for the Hall of Heroes!"

"Dear me. One tub of water does not a warrior make." And she tried to laugh as she took my cup of cocoa from the end table and handed it to me. But her hand shook. She tried to steady it with her other hand, and that made the shaking worse instead of better. She set the cup down. "Perhaps I should let you get it," she said. I took the cup from the table.

"Are you sick again?" I asked her.

"Sit by me dear. Be careful. It's hot," she said.

I sat down. "Are you sick?" I asked again.

"My, Jean," she exclaimed softly in her Georgia accent. "Do I look like I'm sick?"

"It's just that you're in your robe. And your hands are shaking." I would have left it at that, but when she looked at me, I saw something that I recognized. It was hard to remember at first, but then I did. There was a look around her eyes--not dark circles, though they were beginning. It was a look of being sick or being in pain. When I'd first known her I hadn't noticed it much. But now that it was back, I did

115

see it for what it was. "Miss Harris, you are sick," I said. "I don't have to stay if you'd rather be in bed."

"You're so perceptive for being just eleven," she exclaimed. She wasn't mad or impatient. She seemed amazed that I would have noticed such a thing. For a moment all we did was look at each other. I was just surprised that she'd gotten sick again. And that dumping two tubs of water out a window would make her tired enough to tremble and lose her breath. I was trying to figure out what could be wrong with her and if she should go to the doctor. And it did occur to me that if Miss Harris did get sick, that awful nurse would come back.

But at last her expression softened. Miss Harris was very beautiful. Her eyes made up a big part of her face, and they said a lot. She took my china cup out of my hands. And now her hands were more steady and sure.

"I have to tell you something," she said.

I watched her set the cup down and looked at her. "What?" I asked.

For a moment she said nothing. I saw for sure, as I watched her eyes, that she was in some kind of pain, and that the dark circles under her eyes really were coming back. She turned back to look at me.

"Jean," she said very softly. "God brought you to me. I knew that from the beginning. You're very special to Him, and you're very special to me."

She was being so serious that I thought I should be absolutely honest. "I think I know that," I told her. "I mean, about being special to you." It didn't sound very humble to say it, but it was true.

"I've told you before that the Christian's whole life has to be spent learning to fellowship with God, she said. "We learn through so many different adventures--some we might like better than others. Some seem hard at first. " She stopped, looked at me as though realizing that I had no idea what she was saying, and then added, "I'm drinking from a cup that Christ drank of, Jean."

I shook my head. "What does that mean? Just tell me what you have to tell me."

"I have cancer," she told me.

I only looked at her for a moment. Cancer's a big word, and it means a lot of things. It sure meant a lot of things to me just then. It may seem odd, but the first thing that I asked was, "Skin cancer?"

"It no longer matters what kind of cancer, Jean. Because it has metastasized. Do you know what that means?"

"No, I don't know," I told her. It was true, I didn't. But I felt my eyes fill with tears. Just the way she'd said the words told me everything. "Are you going to die?" I asked.

"Everybody dies. None of us knows when--" she began.

"Yes you do!" I exclaimed. "Are you telling me that you're going to die? " I almost yelled it at her, which isn't right to do, but I thought it was so unfair of her not to just say it if it was true.

She was taken back for a second. But at last she said, "If things follow their normal course, then I will die from it. "

"Soon? " I asked.

"Rather soon. Sooner than I would choose otherwise. "

I felt tears sting my eyes again, and I said, "Are you scared? " And my voice faltered, even though I didn't mean for it too. In fact, the only thing I really felt was that it would be terrible to let her see how much it scared me, because that would only make it worse and make me seem like a big baby. But I couldn't help it. I caught my breath back in a sob.

She gently and kindly moved closer and put her arms around me, settled my head against her shoulder, and put her own head against mine.

"It doesn't mean that God has lost control of the situation," she said. "It doesn't mean He loves me less. It means that I have a separate calling. Only Christ can walk with me where I must walk, Jean."

"Why didn't you tell me?" I demanded, and then I burst out crying. I wasn't just sad; I was mad, too. And not just at God. It almost felt like she had been lying to me all along. Because of course now I realized that she had been sick with cancer ever since I had first met her. "Why didn't you tell me before?" I demanded. "Why didn't you tell me when you were sick before?"

"Forgive me," she asked me. "Please forgive me, Jean. I didn't mean to hide things from you. "

That made it worse. I mean, it made me cry more. But I nodded under her head so that she could feel it that I did forgive her. Then she said, "The cancer has gone into remission four times, Jean. Four times. I was diagnosed with it before I ever went to Africa. There was a chance this time that it would go into remission again. I was sick last month--not so much from the cancer as from the chemo-therapy."

I calmed down as she explained it. I sat up again. "Is it the chemo-therapy now?" I asked her.

"Well, yes, in part," she said. "My stomach is upset, and I feel a little dizzy from a new therapy that I've started. I don't go to the hospital for this. It's an oral type of chemo-therapy. But I'll be honest with you, the cancer itself causes some pain. I'll probably be in pain from now on." She looked down at me. "Forgive me, Jean. There are no books of etiquette or procedure for a person with cancer. It was wrong not to tell you; it would have been wrong to tell you needlessly and frighten you."

I had stopped crying, but she asked me, "You will forgive me, won't you?" and I started again.

"Yes!" I exclaimed. "I don't want you to die!"

She hesitated, and I calmed myself down. My outburst of temper--the first one, anyway--was over.

"Listen to me," she said. "All our lives are spent to have fellowship with God, Jean. There's a special fellowship--the fellowship of His sufferings. We can know Him in that way, by suffering as He suffered. That's my calling, Jean."

"I don't want that calling," I said.

"Nobody has laid it on you," she told me. "It's a hard calling, but I haven't lost the joy of my salvation in it. No, I've gained joy. I've gained more understanding in prayer. It's so different from what I thought, Jean. Believe me when I say it." She handed me my cup again. "I wouldn't have laid this calling on myself, Jean. I never had the strength to ask for it. But now that it's mine, I can be thankful."

I didn't have anything to say about callings just then. I didn't look at her for a second, and I gulped my hot cocoa. She was almost a stranger in our town, just about alone except for me. I felt sorry for her, and I wondered why God would leave her so alone at a time like this.

I don't think she read my thoughts or anything, but it wasn't just a coincidence when she said at last, "You've brought me such joy, Jean." She stroked my hair. "That's how I knew you were special to God. Because He had you waiting here for me, and you've brought me so much joy."

There was a lot I had to ask her. I had to know more about what this kind of cancer was, and what it did. I had to know if there was still any chance it would go into remission. I had to know how long she would live if it didn't go into remission. I had to make sure she wasn't afraid, and I wanted to make sure that it wouldn't hurt.

"Are you scared? " I asked her at last. She hadn't really answered me yet.

"Oh," she said quickly, as though to cover for herself for a moment. Then more deliberately,

"Sometimes I'm afraid, Jean. But maybe I'm afraid of things that you aren't thinking of. I'm not afraid to go to heaven. I hardly think about the action of dying itself. It's what comes before, " she said, and she stopped.

I was too afraid to ask her. I didn't want to know what came before. So at first I didn't know what to say, and then I asked, "Can I help you? " My voice-- even to me--sounded very small. It seems, when somebody who has a doctorate and has traveled all over the world and translated the Bible has cancer, that there won't be much that you can do for her if you are only eleven years old and don't even know entirely how cancer works and what it does. To my surprise, she let out a laugh that also sounded like she might start to cry, and then she looked at me with wet eyes and a smile that was trembly.

"You always help me, " she said. "Don't be afraid of me because I have cancer, Jean. After all, I've had it ever since you've known me. It doesn't change me. "

"I'm not afraid of you," I told her. "You're my best friend. "

"Oh Jean, thank you, " she whispered earnestly, "God has made you gracious."

"Just tell me if maybe God would heal you or make it go into remission?" I asked her. "If we prayed real hard."

"He has shown me, Jean, that I must--and will--die of cancer," she said. "As for this time around, it doesn't seem like it's going to go into remission again. But even remission would have been only temporary, He has promised to bear me through all that comes." She kissed me and then put her cheek alongside mine. "Courage comes with knowing God," she whispered.

I nodded, finished the cocoa, and went to change into my own clothes. For a moment I thought it was too much to take, because the longer I thought about it the more I realized that she was my best friend. But then I shook those feelings away. I had to take it. The Lord had made me her Young Helps person. He had a purpose. I was part of the plan.

Chapter 14: The Attempt at a Rescue

 Mom was ironing when I got home. As soon as she saw me, she said, "Jean, what's wrong?" She set the iron at rest on the end of the board.

"Martha Harris has cancer," I told her. "She's going to die from it."

She came round the board and put her hand on my shoulder. "What? Are you sure, Jean? Did she say that?"

"I asked her. It's because it's metastasized. Do you know what that means?" And, mostly because Mom was so serious about it, my eyes filled up with tears.

"When cancer metastasizes, that means it's moved into other parts of the body," she told me. "Honey, I'm sorry." And she hugged me. "No wonder she came home from the mission field. We should have done more to help her."

"Well, I've been cleaning."

"I mean the church should have done more to see to her care," Mom said. "That's part of the function of a church."

"It is?"

"Yes, it certainly is. Mr. Orlando is a good man, but I'm not sure he knows the complete situation. I'll give him a call." She brushed aside my bangs and looked at my eyes. "Everybody's gone skating, but there's going to be a meeting of the Hall of Heroes here at four."

"I'll wait for them," I said. "I don't feel like skating."

When the others came back and we started the meeting, I told them about my news. They were nice about it. I told them that Mom had said the church would help Miss Harris, and Suzette said, "It's good that the church is going to help her," like that was all there was. And Curtis said, "Maybe she'll get better anyway. Sometimes the doctors are wrong."

But Digger said, "Could I go with you next week, Jean? Maybe I can do some fix up work for her."

Digger did a lot of work for his grandmother, and he had his own box of tools.

"Sure," I told him. "The kitchen faucet never stops dripping, and there's a door in the hallway that she can't get open. She says the lock froze."

He nodded. "I can probably fix those."

Talk turned to the missing clubhouse. We wanted to get it back, even me. And Digger had news.

"Eddy's friend, Gary," he said. "The tall one. He's got an uncle who has a house out of town on the other side of the lake. His uncle's always out driving long distance, and Gary sneaks over there all the time to hide stuff." He looked at all of us. "The runner tracks were going off in that direction. The shed could be over there."

Curt was unsure. "You think they could hide a whole shed over there?"

Digger nodded. "Yeah, I do. It's a couple acres, and some of it's wooded. The shed's over there somewhere."

"Well you can bet the three of them are going to keep an eye on it," Suzette said. "They're probably camping in it if it's over there. We can't just go over and tell them to give it back to us."

"Even they're not stupid enough to camp in a metal shed," Rebecca told her. "Not in this weather."

"I know those guys aren't going to sit watch in the dead cold of early morning," Digger said. "We ought to get up at four on Saturday morning. We could find it by five or six and drag it back while they're all sleeping."

"A coup for us!" I exclaimed. And if the search took place in the early morning on Saturday, I would be able to go and still get to Martha Harris's by early afternoon. Then I realized that I'd forgotten to tell them about my own run-in with Eddy's bunch. I told them what happened that morning.

"I'd like to stick their faces in the slush," Curtis said.

Digger had a half smile on his face at the thought of a tub of water dropping onto them. "Miss Harris sounds brave enough to be in the Hall of Heroes."

"I think she's really brave," I told him. "She's braver than all of us."

"What?" Curtis asked.

* * * *

Waking up at four in the morning in the winter wasn't much fun. The cold felt twice as cold, even though there wasn't any wind. We only had two flashlights at our house, and Curt and Rebecca said they ought to hold them. I didn't argue. I wanted to keep my hands in my coat pockets, even with mittens on, and stay hunched down as much as possible. In fact, I didn't even want to go at that point. But I had said I would, and I was pretty sure I'd be glad later that I'd played my part. When you're the youngest, it's always smart to get in when you can.

Rebecca acted like it was just another thing for us to do, like skating or going to the shopping center together. She'd laid out clothes for both of us in our room, and she let me use the bathroom first. But Curtis was in a bad mood. He pulled his clothes on without combing his hair or washing his face, and most of his hair stood straight up and was full of static. He jammed his knit cap on over everything.

We got out of the house by four thirty and trudged through the darkness and glimmering snow to meet Digger and Suzette at the corner of our street. Digger was already waiting for us, but Suzette was no where in sight. So we waited for her until nearly five, and then Digger said we ought to go without her and she wasn't coming anyway.

I felt bad for her and didn't like to think about her rushing to catch up to us if she'd accidentally overslept. That was the sort of thing I might do. Then it would hurt her feelings if we left without her. But Curtis said Suzette was never going to get out of bed this early, and we should stick to the plan. And even Rebecca said it looked like she wasn't coming. But just as we would have gone, Suzette came running up the street, waving to tell us she was here.

"She runs like a girl," Curt complained.

"She's walking now," I told him.

By then we were thirty minutes later than we'd planned, and the boys were mad at Suzette. We trudged off towards the lake. "Why are you guys so grumpy?" Suzette asked. "Getting up early's not so bad if you go to bed early."

When the sun is out and everybody's going skating, the walk to the lake seems like a quick thing. But when it's numbingly cold and dark and lonely, the walk seems a lot longer.

We crossed the silent and frozen lake. By that time, the walking had warmed me up, and I was more interested in looking around. Curtis seemed determined to be miserable, and---for once---Rebecca was too annoyed with Suzette to cover for her. Rebecca's never late for anything, and I was sure she thought it was just plain rude of Suzette to keep us waiting in the cold.

So then, of course, Suzette started being nice to me, because everybody who mattered was mad at her. She asked me if I wanted to hold her flashlight for a while. But I said no, I wanted to keep my hands in my pockets. I tried to say it nicely. I didn't want to argue with her. After all of this, I just wanted to find the shed.

The sun wasn't really coming up yet, but the sky wasn't as pitch black as it had been. We left the far side of the lake and started up a double rutted, snowy road.

"His uncle's house is up in that direction," Digger said, pointing ahead and to our left. "Watch for a turn-off. It might not be plowed out."

We walked for another few minutes and then found the turn off. By now we were in the woods, all right. But we could smell wood smoke from a fireplace. And the sky above was getting that powdery blue look as dawn inched closer. The houses out here were spread far apart in cleared lots among the slender trees. It wasn't a dark forest like you read about in books. The trees were spindly trees, the kind that put out leaves in the spring, not evergreen. It was mostly birch.

We toiled along, and then Digger stopped in amazement. "Look!" he said. We followed his pointing finger. To our amazement, there were fresh tracks of two runners in the snow. They joined the route we were on from another unplowed lane through the trees. The runners had pressed down the boot prints of the people who had been pulling the load along, but we could see the direction to follow.

"This is great!" Digger said. "They must have moved it just yesterday. Come on. Single file, and everybody stay quiet. We must be close to the house."

We did as he said, and of course I was last in line. But we were all excited and happy, now. Everybody switched off their flashlights, which were pretty unnecessary by this time anyway, and we followed Digger as he followed the track of the runners.

We came to a big, open lot. When Digger had said Gary's uncle was a long distance truck driver and had a house out in the woods, I had imagined a dingy little shack. But we saw a big, roomy house with lots of windows, sitting on a rise of ground. There was a blanket of snow over everything, but you could see long indentations where a few flower beds had been put in. Much closer to us, down at the foot of the wide open space, there was a long, single-story building with only one tiny window in it. It was made of wood, very sturdy, but clearly not a house. I guessed it was a machine shed for snow mobiles and the lawn tractor. Thick snow lay on the roof, a couple feet of it. Where we live, people have to sweep off roofs once or twice each winter, and this one must have been swept once already since the snows had started.

The runner tracks moved along the side of this building, as though the people pulling our clubhouse had walked along the side of it furthest from the big house and then crossed the large open place, moving towards the trees on the other side of the clearing.

Digger must have decided that this was the best way to move, because it would keep us out of sight of the house for as long as possible. He motioned for us to be quiet, and we started across the lower end of the open lot. We came into the sheltered side of the long low building.

Digger paused long enough to peek into the tiny window just to make sure we wouldn't be seen, but then he nodded and gestured for us to come along. He had just reached the end of the long building with all of us behind him and was peeking around the corner when we heard somebody yell, "Now! Push! Push!"

Two things happened at once. A huge mountain of snow came straight down on us from the roof of the building, and Eddy himself leaped out in front of Digger with the biggest power hose I'd ever seen in his hands. I had one glimpse of it, and then we all got hit by a wall of water.

I was in the back of the line, so I got hit the least, both from the snow and the water. But whoever was up on the roof kept pushing the drifts of snow down on the people beneath. I had one glimpse of two boys up there with wide push brooms. Then I took to my heels and ran for the woods. Curtis passed me, and Rebecca passed me, and then I stopped and saw that Digger had pulled up Suzette by her bulky coat. She was furious, and she didn't want to run, which made it worse because they were getting blasted by the water. I think she wanted Digger to turn and fight them all. But he quit arguing and just pulled her after himself, and then at last she ran after him, and she was yelling at him.

I decided that the littlest person better just run, because those goons might just catch me. So I ran and let Digger and Suzette look after themselves.

We heard them laughing at us, but Eddy stopped when he got the hose to its full length and couldn't chase us with it any further.

We ran all the way back to the frozen lake, and then we slowed to a walk and caught our breath. But we didn't stop to rest.

As Suzette got her breath back, she started yelling at Digger again. She said a man should fight to defend a woman, especially if there was only one man in front of him. Then she started blaming him for having made such a stupid plan in the first place. Digger didn't say anything through all of this, but I could see he was mad at her.

"You can come over to our house," Rebecca told him. We knew if he went home all wet, his grandmother would give him the silent treatment. Digger's grandmother never yelled at him, but she would ignore him and wouldn't speak to him if she thought he had done something wrong.

We also knew that was why he didn't yell back at Suzette. Digger always had to be careful because, even if he sometimes had a hard time with his grandmother, he wanted to stay with her. So he never made trouble.

"You always take his side!" Suzette exclaimed, angry because nobody felt sorry for her.

"You were the one who was too stupid to run!" Curtis shouted. "You just stood there and got blasted by that hose. I'd have left you there!"

"You did leave me there!" she yelled back. "At least Digger helped me, even if he wouldn't fight them."

"Stop calling names!' Rebecca said. "It's over and done. Suzette, you'd better get home before you get sick. I'll call you later."

"What are you guys going to do?" she asked.

"Dry off!" Curtis exclaimed.

Then everybody was silent. When we got to the corner, Suzette went her way and the rest of us went our way. But Curtis and I were hardly wet at all, so we volunteered to buy doughnuts at the place around the corner and meet Digger and Rebecca at home.

By the time we got home with two bags of white powdered doughnuts, we felt better. Digger had hung up his wet coat and outer things. Otherwise, only his jeans were wet. He sat at the kitchen table in one of my Dad's old robes, having coffee like a grown up while my Dad cooked up eggs. Everybody else was in bed. Rebecca came out in a few minutes in dry clothes. Pretty soon we were all settled down with doughnuts and hot chocolate, while Dad had eggs, and the day didn't seem too bad. I mean, we'd gotten trounced by the Reinbach gang, but there's a lot to be said for doughnuts and hot chocolate on Saturday morning when everybody else is in bed. Only Curtis was still mad.

In our family, after me, there's a five year gap and then my little brother Peter is next, and after him the youngest, my sister Noelle. They don't come into the story much. That morning while everything dried we played with them, and then we tried a game of Monopoly. Digger and Rebecca are pretty good about making the little ones feel like they're playing, too.

Since Monopoly is the longest game ever invented, by the time we finished and Curtis had won like he always does, everything was dry enough. We had lunch, and then Digger and I went over to his house to get his tools and from there we went to see Miss Harris.

She was dressed for the day, though by now I could see that she wasn't feeling entirely well. But she welcomed us, and we got right to work. I dusted and vacuumed, and Digger went to the door that was stuck fast. He opened his tool box and took the doorknob off, but he still couldn't get the door open. So he took off the hinges. I helped him lift the door away.

The closet held only some old coats and hats and a few boxes. Digger said he could put in a new doorknob if he took the old one to the hardware store. So he put on his coat and hat and left to run that errand while I did the dishes. Miss Harris told me that she would wait for me on the sofa. I knew she wasn't feeling well. So after she dozed off, I cleaned the downstairs bathroom for her.

I realized that she had always done that herself because she sometimes got sick from her medication, and she didn't want to make me clean up where she had been sick. But after you've changed diapers, how bad can anything be? There was no shower or tub in the downstairs bathroom. I cleaned the toilet and sink as hard as I could, washed my hands, and changed the hand towels. Then I shook out the small square rug and put it back. I could have mopped the floor, but just then Digger came back, and he needed my help.

She woke up while we were getting the door back on its hinges.

"You've been so busy," she said. "Shall I make cocoa for you?"

"Yes, thank you," Digger said. The afternoon was getting away. "But if I hurry, I can fix the kitchen faucet for you," he added.

She stopped before she entered the kitchen and turned to him. "But if you fix everything today, Digger, you may never come back."

He was on his knees, trying to fit the hinges together, and he looked up and grinned with the easiest, happiest grin I'd ever seen on his face. "Miss

Harris, there's plenty to do here. I'll be back next week if you want."

"Thank you. Jean has spoken so highly of you that I have to reserve some time for all of us to get acquainted." She smiled. And she went into the kitchen.

He glanced at me. "You didn't tell her about the ambush this morning?"

"She's been napping," I said. Then I warned him. "She's probably going to think it's funny."

"It is funny."

While we put milk on the stove to heat, Digger fixed the faucet. Miss Harris had beautiful china cups that I liked to use, but she found a very big mug for Digger. I carried the cups out to the living room: cocoa for me and tea for her, and then I retrieved Digger's mug and the plate of butter cookies. Digger put all of his tools back in his tool box and carried it out to the front step. I ducked into the kitchen, and while Miss Harris put away the cocoa and sugar, I gave the saucepan a quick scrubbing.

"My, he's such a grown up young man," she said.

I suddenly realized that he'd seemed a lot more grown up that afternoon than he'd ever seemed before. "You're lucky to have such a kind friend," she told me. She put her hands on my shoulders.

"Digger's parents don't love him," I said suddenly. "I don't know why. He has to live with his grandmother."

Her eyes and expression became very serious. We heard him come back inside, and we went out to the living room to visit.

Exactly as I predicted, when we told Miss Harris about what happened that morning, she laughed. But suddenly I thought it was funny too. Digger got more and more lively as he told it, and when he imitated Suzette trying to turn around and yell at Eddy Reinbach while Eddy was blasting her with a high powered hose, I fell back laughing. Miss Harris had tears in her eyes, and she was holding herself.

"Digger, you've got to stop," she gasped. "It hurts if I laugh too hard."

The time had flown by. Digger and I carried the cups and plate back to the kitchen and found our coats. Martha Harris wrapped my scarf for me, and then she did the same for Digger, and she said, "You will see Jean home and look after her, Digger?"

Digger's eyes were suddenly solemn, and his voice was soft. "Yes," he said. "Of course."

It was snowing again. As we started down the walk, Mrs. Everett, the nurse, pulled up. Miss Harris had already closed the door. I was pretty sure that she had felt very unwell all afternoon, but she had pulled up all her strength to see us. In a sense I was glad the nurse had come. Digger and I made way for her on the walk, but she stopped and said, "So there are two of you now?"

Digger glanced from me to her.

"We've been cleaning and fixing things for Miss Harris," I said.

"You should have one of your parents here to keep you in order," she told us.

143

Neither one of us said anything. I'd already learned from Digger just to keep my mouth shut to avoid trouble. But Mrs. Everett didn't like this. She gave us a long lecture about what we should and shouldn't do when we were in another person's house. And she told us not to bring our noisy friends over. And she told us we should confine our visits to an hour, and come separately.

After she let us go, Digger only glanced at me, puzzled.

"That's the nurse," I told him. "I don't think she likes kids."

We'd told our Dad the latest on the shed, and when I got home that night, I found Officer Franks at the house, talking with Dad. Our town has only a few policemen on the force.

Officer Franks was a big man who wore a big belt with a gun and a radio. There was a slot for a night stick, but he'd left it in his car. He'd once commented that in our town the police would be better armed with jumper cables than weapons.

His visit was sort of informal, a drop-in just to update Dad.

After I'd said hello to him, he told Dad, "We can follow up on searching for the shed out across the lake. I don't mind telling you that Eddy Reinbach and his friends are pretty well known in all the local stores for their shoplifting. I don't doubt they stole it. But finding it is another matter. But we'll go out and have a look."

But the snow was falling pretty thickly. In another couple hours, the runner tracks would be gone.

Chapter 15: The Quest for the Hall

Mom and Dad gave me permission to see Miss Harris during the week. She wasn't able to come to the prayer meeting at church on Wednesday night any more, so Mom and Dad dropped me off at her house on the way to church and picked me up afterward. At first Curtis was really mad that I got to spend the Wednesday evenings at Miss Harris' and have cocoa and cookies while he had to go to church. He complained about it the first night that I went over to her house. He sat in the car with his arms folded and said it wasn't fair.

But I told him that Miss Harris and I were studying the Bible together. And we prayed together. And Dad put his foot down. He glanced into the rear view mirror at Curt for a second as he drove. "Jean gives up every Saturday afternoon to be a servant to Martha Harris, and now her service gives her a certain liberty. If she were going over there just to have chocolate and cookies, it would be one thing. But it's more important than that." He glanced at me. "Am I right, Jean?"

I nodded.

"That's the law of love, Curtis," Mom told him. "Going to church doesn't make a person good, and it doesn't fill a person with love. But when a person experiences the grace of God and works in the spirit of love, everything the person does in love is part of Christian growth."

"You mean God wants Jean at Martha Harris's instead of church?" Curtis asked.

"For now, yes," Mom said.

I just kept my mouth shut during the argument. I knew Curtis would never agree anyway, and I was just glad---and surprised---that I was allowed to spend Wednesday evenings with Miss Harris. We were studying the Gospel of John together, and she would show me some of the Greek words in the squiggly writing of real Greek, and then she would show me other places in the Bible where the same words showed up. She would explain how she would say certain verses in other languages and how the words would have to clarify meanings.

In John 10:30, when the Lord Jesus says "I and my Father are one," some cultures believe that every human being is a part of God, so they wouldn't see the verse as being important if it were translated without being more specific. To people who grow up believing that God is in all of us, Jesus would simply be claiming that He's enlightened. She showed me that for some Chinese languages, the way the verse is translated emphasizes the Greek meaning that the divine Father is a separate, distinct God, and Christ is the same, separate person as the divine Father. So to the Chinese, the verse would be translated more like "I and the Divine Father are the same one," for people of that culture to understand the original meaning.

I realized that to translate the Bible into other languages, a person would have to know languages, cultures, and the way people think. I could hardly believe that Miss Harris had figured all of this out.

What was even more amazing was that we could talk about the way adjectives work or how to get nouns to turn into verbs, and it was interesting. It wasn't like doing grammar in school or sitting down to do homework.

As a few weeks went by, there were good nights when we studied together and she explained things to me, and there were some nights when we sat on the sofa together and I read the Bible to her because she didn't feel well.

One Wednesday night when Dad pulled up the long, narrow path that was her driveway, we saw an unfamiliar car parked by the house. It was an old car, but it had been washed and waxed and didn't have any of the grime from old snow, sand, and salt on it.

"Looks like Miss Harris has company," Dad said.

I scrambled out and went up to the door. When I knocked, a tall black man in a suit and tie answered. He beamed down at me as though we knew each other. "Hello, little girl!" he exclaimed in a deep voice, with an accent. "Have you lost your way? Or have you come to see Dr. Harris?"

Martha called from the living room, and we entered. There were stacks and stacks of papers everywhere. Everything was tidy and looked organized, but she and this man had obviously been working on something.

"Oh Jean," she said as we came in. "I'm afraid that I forgot you were coming tonight, dear."

The man looked down at me. "Are you a good friend to Dr. Harris, little girl?"

"This is Jean, my dear friend," Martha told him. "Jean, this is Dr. Josef."

"How do you do?" I asked him, and I held out my hand. His skin was as dark as coffee beans, and his voice was deep and different. Rich. Happy. He seemed mysterious and yet friendly. I liked him, but he was the sort of man you call "sir" even if nobody tells you to.

"I am very well, Miss Jean, thank you," he told me. He shook hands with me, and his hand was huge. "You must come in and have a seat. I am delighted to meet a good friend to Dr. Harris."

He had brought in a chair from the kitchen so that he could face Miss Harris on the sofa. Most of the stacks of papers were arranged around his chair. It looked to me like they had been going over the papers together.

I picked my way between the stacks and sat next to Miss Harris. But I could hardly take my eyes off of him. He sat down in the chair and smiled at me, and I liked his smile.

"Dr. Josef is the Director of the translation project," Martha Harris told me. "He's been on a lecture tour for a couple months, and we've been going over the proofs of our latest work."

"You're from Africa?" I asked him.

He smiled again. "I was born in Kenya, Miss Jean, but I grew up in England. I went to school at Oxford."

"That's where Latimer and Ridley were burned!" I exclaimed.

His eyes lit up with surprise, and suddenly I realized that he liked me, too. "Yes, my dear, but that happened a few years before I arrived." He straightened up and then sat back in the hard chair. "How does a little American girl like you know about two great martyrs for the Word of God?" he asked. "Do you know our Lord and Savior Jesus Christ, Miss Jean?"

From any other person, that might have sounded awkward to say, but from him, it wasn't.

"Yes," I told him. "Miss Harris has told me about Tyndale and Erasmus and a lot of those men."

He nodded. "So you know how important it is to translate God's Word. We have been very busy all day, for I have a rare opportunity to see Dr. Harris face to face and consult her knowledge." He made his voice persuasive and kind. "Will you help us as we work together?"

"Can I get you some coffee or hot cocoa, Dr. Josef?" I asked him. A smile that I didn't understand spread across Martha's face, and Dr. Josef suddenly grinned at me.

He held out his watch so that I could see it. "In one hour, I would welcome some hot cocoa, Miss Jean. Can you give us one hour together to finish our day's work?"

I realized that Dr. Josef thought I was younger than I actually was. Of course I could wait for an hour. But I wasn't annoyed with him. He was trying to be nice to me, and I realized that they were very concerned about their work.

"Do you mind doing the Bible study at the kitchen table?" Miss Harris asked me.

"No, I don't mind," I said. "I want your work to go well."

"Thank you, Miss Jean, I promise you, we will take no longer than one hour," he said.

So I sat at the kitchen table and worked on the Bible study and answered the questions at the end of the chapter. But from the living room, I could hear them. I finished the workbook, and then I just listened. Some of what they were saying went over my head. For one thing, they would ask each other about long phrases in other languages. And sometimes even when they spoke in English, the words were too technical.

But as the conversation got more intense, I heard him say, "It still doesn't solve the problem they have with atonement, Martha dear. Even worded that way, many will still see in the phrase that God is subject to evil. In their language, atonement and placating are nearly equivalent."

"I would still resist outright paraphrasing," Martha's calm, slow voice answered. "Can we embed a borrowed word?"

Then they went off into more technical talk. It seemed, from what they were saying, that the people who would read the translation thought that atoning for sin meant having to quiet evil spirits by giving the spirits blood. So the Bible's message of God sending His son to be the atonement for our sins---to those people--- would mean that God had to placate evil spirits. Their own language and religious background would confuse the original meaning of the Bible.

I considered the problem for myself. Somehow the translators would have to make the readers understand that atonement was different from placating. I tried to decide for myself how the two ideas were different.

Their discussion continued. At one point, Martha said, "It might be solved by the verbs. The wording should emphasize that it is God who demands atonement. So the action of atoning, carried through the verb, is to God. God receives the action."

"We shall look at the passage in Hebrews again," Dr. Josef said, and there was more shuffling of papers.

Their discussion went on for more than an hour, but I didn't mind. After ninety minutes had passed, Dr. Josef said, "Oh Martha dear, you are as white as the snow. We're finished."

And then she said, "I'm all right. I wonder what Jean is doing. She may have fallen asleep at the table."

His big footsteps crossed the floor, and then I saw him down the hall. "There is Miss Jean!" he exclaimed. "You've been a good girl! Did you fall asleep, my dear?"

I stood up. "No. I hope you don't mind. I was listening."

He came up the hall. "Oh! So you are interested in our work? Do you like the study of language?"

"I don't know," I told him. "I think so. I don't know if I could learn all of that."

With that king-like ease of his, he went right to the cupboard where the pots and pans were kept. He pulled down a sauce pan and found the tin of cocoa powder. I got the milk.

"How old are you, Miss Jean?" he asked.

"Eleven. But I've never taken a foreign language."

I passed him the milk, and he poured it into the sauce pan. "Yes, it takes years and years to become a translator," he said. "And it is a big job. But it is like the story of Tesshu, the samurai. Do you know what a samurai is?"

I nodded. "A warrior from Japan."

He smiled and put the milk on the burner. "Well Tesshu was a great man in his way, although he did not know the Lord. But when he was old, he decided that he would copy all of the Buddhist writings over into his written language. There were thousands of pages. In fact, the old writings filled up an entire room! And his friends said, 'Lord Tesshu! It will be too hard for you! It is far too hard even for a great samurai like you to copy all of these writings!"

"What did he say?" I asked.

Dr. Josef smiled, and his eyes lit up, as though he really liked this samurai. "Tesshu said, "Don't be silly! It isn't too hard at all. For I shall copy only one page at a time.'"

He looked down at me and saw that I didn't get it. "Nobody can truly say, 'Now I will do this or now I will be this,'" he told me. "We attend to everything only one page at a time. Today you can study the Bible and do well in school and look after your friend Dr. Harris. Today you can pray to God and have fellowship with Him. Today you say, "Look on my heart and lead me in the right way." Then God, in His time, does what He thinks is best. So then, as God works in you, one day you look up and realize you are a translator. Or you are something else. The heart of serving God is that He makes us what He wants us to be. We don't make ourselves."

He passed the milk carton back to me. "Do you understand?"

"Yes," I said. "Thank you."

As I went to the refrigerator, he said, "Whoever translates the Word of God spends long hours with God's thoughts, and it is a wonderful calling. But the translation of the Word of God is always under the attack of Satan. We oppose the world, the flesh, and the devil, Miss Jean. It is a costly calling."

I felt very sobered by this. "Is that why Miss Harris has cancer?" I asked him.

"I don't know." He stirred the milk. "I do know that God has willed her sickness for His good purpose, and Satan will use it for his own purpose. If he can throw darts of deadly illness into the spreading of God's Word, he will do so. But God will win in the end." He wasn't smiling now, but he wasn't sad, either. He looked down at me again. "We have only today, and today Dr. Harris is translating God's Word. Tomorrow, the Lord may return, and then what does sickness matter?"

   * * * *

After Dr. Josef left, Miss Harris seemed to take a turn for the worst. When Digger and I came the next Saturday she didn't even come out of her room until the very end, and then she said very little, though she thanked us for our work and finished up the day by wrapping our scarves for us and asking Digger to walk me home and look after me.

The next Wednesday night, she asked me to read to her from our passage in John, so I did. I sat next to her on the sofa, but as I read, she turned her head to look at the pictures on the wall, especially the series of pictures from the children's home in Africa.

After I finished the chapter, she didn't say anything, so I waited. She still had her head turned away, towards the pictures. It almost seemed like she was ignoring me, or just trying to shut out everything. I didn't think she could be doing that, and at last I said, "Maybe we could send them some toys or something, through the church."

She let out a hard, impatient sigh like I'd never heard from her. "What would they do with toys, Jean?" she asked. She turned to me, and her face was like I'd never seen it. Not angry, but sarcastic.

"Should they play like you play, and then go off to a school and come home and eat dinner, clothed and safe and educated? Would all the toys and clothes that you and your brothers and sisters have give them what they need?"

"Well, no," I began. I felt very stupid.

"Maybe you could give them parents and laws and everything else you have that they'll never get." She said it like she was blaming me, accenting the word "you" so that it sounded like it was wrong for me to have what I had.

I don't remember standing up. All I knew next was that I was on my feet, looking at her. And her eyes suddenly got round. I heard myself talk. I don't think I even knew what I would say, but there was my voice, and it didn't sound like me. "I'm going home now," it said.

"Jean, I'm sorry," she gasped.

I turned around and walked out. I went straight to the closet and pulled out my coat. She came to the hallway.

"Stay away from me," I heard myself say.

"I apologize," she said.

"Fine." Now I was coming back to myself. I was about to cry or yell or both. I struggled into my coat.

"You mustn't leave before your parents come get you," she said gravely, but she didn't come any closer. "It isn't safe for you to walk home after dark."

She was right about that. I wasn't allowed to. "I'll sit on the step outside," I said. "You can go back and look at your pictures." And then I started yelling, at a grown up. "Because they're better than me and than all of us! All right? I'll say it for you!" I had never, in all of my life, yelled at a grown up, and certainly not a missionary.

"I didn't mean that," she began.

"Yes you did!" I shouted at her. She walked towards me, and I retreated around the big, heavy table that was still covered with a computer and stacks of papers. I kept it between us. "I don't know what their lives are like, or how to read their language or how to read the Bible the right way. I don't know anything! Just say that while you're at it!"

"I was unjust, and I'm sorry," she told me.

"It's true! You were supposed to explain it to me!" I shouted. That stopped her. Suddenly something really hot swept over me. It was like all of a sudden I understood more than I'd ever understood before. "I can't help being born here any more than they could help being born there! How dare you blame me for it! How would you feel if I blamed you for having cancer?"

I had to stop shouting at her, and suddenly I realized I wouldn't stop if I didn't close my mouth. So I did. I clapped my mouth closed. She stopped trying to come closer. She seemed stunned by what I'd said. And then I felt a sob rush through me, where the heat had been, and then I cried. But she knew if she came around the table, I would move away from her. For a minute we just stood there, with me crying and trying not to.

"You've told me the truth about myself," she said at last. "And I haven't wronged you alone, but God as well, because He has His hand on your life, and I dared to take Him lightly."

I calmed down. I was still furious, but I got control of myself.

"Do you still want to leave?" she asked me.

"Yes!"

"Jean, you have to promise me that you won't walk home at this hour."

"All right."

"You may sit on the stairs and wait for your parents if you like. If you're not comfortable with me."

I ducked my head. "Okay."

She moved away from the table, back into the hallway, towards the stairs, so that I could come and sit on the lower steps. I came out then.

But something was nudging me. Even though I had felt like I'd understood things better when I was so hot and angry, now that I was cooler and more sad, I realized that she was sad because Dr. Josef was gone. All her work was over for her, even if it wasn't finished. Everything she had loved to do was gone, and here she was, all alone in this snowy town.

As she would have gone into the living room and I was at the foot of the stairway, she said again, more softly, "I have wronged you, Jean, and I do ask you to forgive me."

"Yes, I forgive you," I said. "I'm sorry I yelled at you."

She paused, uncertain if I wanted her to leave me alone or if I wanted us to make friends again.

I sat down on the second step and looked at her.

"Would you like to come back to the living room?" she asked me.

In my entire life, I had never been that angry before, and at last it was going away. When she looked down at me, I felt big tears come to my eyes, and I was almost relieved. These felt more normal: hurt feelings. Just normal hurt feelings. I looked up at her and didn't know what to say. Big tears kept rolling down my cheeks. Believe me, if Dr. Martha Harris wants you to feel stupid, you'll feel stupid. I felt like I'd never be able to live up to her, not if she demanded that I should.

She held out her hand to me. "Please," she said. "We'll pray together. I'll ask God to forgive me."

I nodded and stood up. I didn't take her hand, but I pulled off my coat and left it there. We went into the living room and sat on the sofa, and she prayed. I won't write most of what she prayed about hurting my feelings, but I can say she understood more than I'd realized about all of the new things I'd been thinking over the last several weeks. As she prayed, I realized she was truly sorry, and I realized she hadn't really meant to be that angry with me. She had been angry, probably with God, and she'd taken it out on me. But ending up here had never been a part of her plans. It made her feel lonely to be reminded of Africa and her work there.

As she went on, I came closer until I pushed into her, and she put her arms around me, and we both cried. I had to know that she wanted me to be her friend, but at the same time I was afraid of how angry I had gotten. It scared me. She rocked me like I was younger than what I was, but I didn't mind.

For some reason Dad was a little later than usual that night, and by the end of the evening we were friends again. I decided never to say anything about it to anybody.

* * * *

The Saturday work also went on for several weeks. From the first week, Digger did everything that he could for Martha Harris. He anchored himself to the upstairs window frames and swept the roof for her, then shoveled out that long driveway and the front walk. He set traps in the attic and carried out so many mice that he finally went to the store and put down baits. He got her washing machine to stop "walking" every time it started its spin cycle.

I had been cleaning as best as I could for her, but Digger went upstairs and scraped out all the old caulking and grout in the big bathroom. It took him all of one Saturday afternoon to do it. And he re-caulked everything, then scrubbed the bathroom floor very hard and cut a piece of Berber rug that was a "remnant" to fit the floor. He put down a sheet of rubbery material first that he called a carpet pad, and then he put down the carpet and trimmed it so that it fit perfectly around the toilet and the sink piping. We didn't think paint fumes would be good for her to breathe, so instead of painting the bathroom, we just washed the walls and hung a new mirror.

Now I knew why he was called Digger. He visited all the stores and asked what they were throwing away. Then he would dig through everything to find what he could use. He told me he'd been doing that for his grandmother ever since he came. It was how he'd gotten the padding and the carpet remnant for Miss Harris' bathroom, and the manager of the hardware store had given him the new caulk in return for cleaning out the store's back room.

"I've never done a job this big," he told me as we surveyed the bathroom, which was beautiful to look at. "About partway through, I thought I'd never get it done. But here it is," he added.

"I think you could do anything," I told him. People talk about cleaning as being "women's work," but Digger was a lot stronger than I was, and he could scrub harder and get some things done more quickly. And he didn't mind doing it. Not for Martha Harris, anyway.

And every Saturday afternoon we finished the day by sitting down to hot cocoa and cookies, with Digger drinking from his mug and Miss Harris and I using our china cups. And when we would leave, she would ask him to walk me home and look after me. I thought this was funny, but Digger took it so seriously that I never laughed about it.

Meanwhile, Curtis kept coming up with new plans to find the clubhouse, but every time he set foot on the vacant lots or tried to go down to the lake alone, Eddy and his friends would spot him and pelt him with snow and slush. In fact, all of us were getting pelted pretty badly when ever we went out alone. They seemed to know the routes we took to go back and forth from Suzette's or Digger's house, and they would catch any of us alone as often as they could. The Hall of Heroes, for sure, was taking a pounding.

Chapter 16: The Super Glue Counter Attack

 I thought, after the Wednesday night before, that Miss Harris and I might be a little awkward with each other on Saturday. But there was a lot to do that day. Digger was out "digging for stuff" that he wanted, and he'd told me not to expect him until three.

When I got to the house, Miss Harris came out to greet me, even though she had not yet finished her time in prayer. She gave me a warm hug, and we smiled at each other, so we would know everything was all right. Then I let her go back to her prayers, and I got busy on my chores.

I'm not sure why, but it was a lot more satisfying to clean at Miss Harris' house than it was to clean at my own. I looked forward to it more, and I did a better job. Mrs. Everett came in that day, shot a glare and a nod at me like that was her duty, and went back to check on Miss Harris. But there wasn't much nursing required.

Digger would be coming by three, so after I vacuumed and dusted and cleaned the downstairs bathroom, I washed up all the dishes. Mrs. Everett was gone by then, and Miss Harris came out to work.

"Oh Jean, you work so hard," she said. "We should make something for Digger. Would you like to stay for supper, Dear?"

"Yes," I told her, and I was glad that she wanted me there.

"Do teen age boys eat cupcakes?" she asked.

"They eat brownies. Can we make brownies?"

Her eyes lighted up. Brownies would be easier and faster than cupcakes.

While we were making them, Digger came with a new gadget called a stud finder. It took him a while to figure out how to use it, but then he and I emptied all of the books from the shelves in the cluttered dining area off the main hallway, and he bolted the high bookcases into the wall with his drill. The whole time we worked, you could smell the brownies.

The books themselves were interesting. There were very old books from a hundred years ago. We started to put them back, but then Miss Harris brought us the brownies, and we all sat at the cluttered table with the high mountains of books and looked at some of them. She knew a lot about history, and I don't mean the boring things. She told us about the Tower of London and how condemned noble people were locked up in there. She told us about one man, a Christian during the Protestant Reformation when Christians were executed for preaching the Bible, whose wife visited him the night before his execution. The wife had so many ladies and serving maids with her, and they were all coming and going so much, and crying so openly, that they confused the men on guard about how many were inside the cell and how many were outside. So then she covered her husband over in a woman's cloak, and he bowed his head and went out weeping with the other women and escaped.

She told us about a man who was so afraid of being executed that he signed a paper that renounced his beliefs, and then he felt so bad about what he'd done, he renounced his renunciation and held the hand that had signed the document in the fire to show that he had the resolution to face fire and death for believing the Bible.

We forgot about the time as we sat there looking at the books with her. Then we realized that the afternoon was over. Miss Harris asked Digger if he would like to stay for dinner, but he said he had to get home. He and I quickly put all the books back, and then he went to get his coat.

Supper was very simple: Martha Harris preferred to eat bland things, so she had rice and applesauce, with chicken on the side. She said that I could have what I liked, and we hunted around until we found enough things to make a stir fry. She showed me how to do it. You have to have everything all lined up to do a stir fry properly: chopped vegetables, chopped meat, cold rice, all the spices, and the soy sauce. And then you have to move very quickly to cook it all.

I was nervous because she has a gas stove, and she turned the flame up all the way, but after she worked the skillet and wooden spoon for a minute or two, I told her I thought I could do it, and she let me.

It worked too. It was delicious. We washed and dried the dishes, and the day was almost over.

"Another happy Saturday," I said as I looked out the kitchen window at the pink shafts of the sunset on the white carpet of snow. "It always goes so fast."

She came and stood next to me and put her arms around me. "Do you like being here, Jean? Using your Saturdays this way?"

I nodded. "Digger and I---we're both better people when we're here," I told her. "I'm better when I'm with you. He is, too." I looked up at her. "It's like I'm older when I'm here." But then I thought she might not make cookies with me any more if I said that, so I added, "Only, it's okay to be the youngest when I'm here, too. And Digger doesn't mind that I'm younger, here."

"No, I want you both the way you are," she said. She held me to herself. "I could never have imagined such a delightful friend."

I knew she still felt bad about last Wednesday, so I said, "I know. I know we're friends."

175

"Come and sit down."

We might have worked on our cross stitching, but I didn't really want to work on mine. I asked her to tell me about Africa and what it had been like. So she showed me pictures from a photo album. She was a good story teller, and I liked looking at pictures with her. She told me about the people that she knew, and the things they did, and the way they lived their lives. But the next thing I knew, I was opening my eyes, and I felt very sleepy. The room was quiet, and I heard the clock ticking. The photo album had been set aside. Martha Harris was smiling down at me, her arms around me, her hand holding my head so it didn't tip over. I was happy to see her face, but I felt self conscious because I had fallen asleep.

"Um, would you like tea?" I asked.

"I want you to stay right here," she said. "You don't have to do anything. Just stay right here. Enjoy your rest."

Then I wasn't self conscious. Only sleepy. My eyes started to close, and I forced them open.

"Sleep if you want to, Jean," she said. "I won't leave you. I'm here."

But I wanted to stay awake because I didn't want the day to be over. If I fell asleep, all the time would pass without my knowing it, and I would have to go home. But I was so tired, I couldn't even say it. I just forced my eyes open again as they started to close.

"There's not enough time," I finally whispered.

Her eyes became solemn. "There's time," she said softly. "You'll be back again. Again and again."

I realized that she was thinking of what hadn't occurred to me. But I didn't say so. My eyes were closing even though I tried to keep them open. She was quiet, and the quietness of the room, her soft breathing, and the ticking of the clock in the hallway all came together with a great peacefulness that wrapped around me. When next I woke up, I was in my own bed at home, in my pajamas and under the covers. It was morning.

* * * *

Winter was slowly ending. We hadn't had a good snow in a while, and most of the big white drifts around town were grimy and blackened. In the afternoons, long streams of water flowed along the curbsides and ran into the gratings.

Of course, we still had a few weeks before bare patches of earth would be a common sight, but it was obvious that Spring would finally come. And there was still plenty of snow and slush for Eddy and his friends to ambush us.

The only time they couldn't get us was on the way home from school because our school got out before their school did. And even so, we noticed that on Tuesdays and Thursdays we never got ambushed by them at all. Rebecca could walk over to Suzette's with impunity, and even I could go where I wanted. Digger's house was also safe.

Finally Curtis called a meeting of the Hall of Heroes at our house one Tuesday. By this time, Curtis was mad at me because, according to him, I'd "gotten Digger to spend Saturdays at Miss Harris's house". As though Digger couldn't think for himself and pick what he wanted to do. But Curtis only said this to me once, and he never dared to say it to Digger.

Somehow, we both knew Digger would get mad if Curtis said it to him.

But with Digger gone on Saturdays, the Hall of Heroes was dwindling. We'd lost our clubhouse; losing me from the Saturday meetings probably wasn't all that bad to the others, but losing Digger was as bad as losing the clubhouse. And furthermore, Eddy and his friends were slaughtering us. Suzette was mad at everybody, and now it was clear that only Rebecca liked her, and none of us could figure out why.

But that Tuesday, everybody agreed to meet. All of us knew that my brother Curtis finds out everything he needs to know. I don't know how he does it. But he's always the person who knows how to get things done. He'd been looking around and asking questions and even spying on Eddy's house for the last few weeks. We knew he would have something to tell us, and probably a plan.

On Tuesday we had a teacher workday in the afternoon at school, so we all got home early. Digger and Suzette went to their houses to get changed and then they came over to meet us.

"I know how to find our shed," Curtis said when we were all gathered around the kitchen table with Smaxcaliber, our mascot.

"How?" Digger asked. He didn't sound unfriendly, but his tone of voice showed that he was just about through with trying to find that shed.

"Officer Franks told us they shoplift like crazy," Curt said. "They go to Woolworth's in town every Thursday when the clerks are putting up stuff for the weekend and doing all the price marking."

"So they shoplift," Suzette said. "Who cares about when they do it?"

"Don't you get it?" Curtis asked, ready to be mad at her.

Rebecca, as usual, spoke up to make it clear to Suzette. "If three of them are shoplifting stuff every Thursday, they've collected up a lot of stolen merchandise. They'll have to store it somewhere."

"Our shed!" Digger exclaimed. "That's what Officer Franks thought! They're storing their stuff in our shed!"

"Once the snow melts, there's no hope of tracking the shed," Curtis said. "Even now, with the ground so soft, I bet they can't drag it around any more to keep hiding it. Where ever it is right now, that's where it will have to stay."

Suzette folded her arms. "Curtis Anderson, I am not going on another hare-brained search to find that clubhouse! One dousing was enough for me, thank you!"

"You can do what you want!" Curtis snapped.

"Stop!" Rebecca exclaimed. She calmed her voice down. "Go on, Curt. How do we find the clubhouse?"

"We stake out Woolworth's ahead of those goons," Curtis said. "We see what they steal, and then we spread out on either side of town and watch for them. We can follow them at a distance and switch off on following them."

Digger was doubtful. "What if they see us?"

"We'll form a dragnet. One group radios to the other group and they switch off. So if they see you and me, all we have to do is walk the other way and tell the girls to pick up the trail," Curtis said.

"Radio?" I asked. "Walkie talkies?"

For answer, Curtis pulled up two walkie talkies from the chair next to him and set them on the kitchen table.

"There's only two," I said.

"That's all I could afford."

Suzette's voice was disgusted. "We should use cell phones."

"The rest of us don't have cell phones," Digger said.

"But there's only two," I said. "There are five of us."

"We'll have to split up into two teams," Curtis said.

"A dragnet made up of only two teams?" I asked. But nobody answered me. Not even Digger. And of course I knew why. Two walkie talkies meant two teams of two each, and the youngest one doesn't get to do anything.

The next Thursday, this was pretty much the way it worked out. Rebecca and Digger made a big deal about telling me that I was the official lookout, and my job was to sit at the soda fountain counter near the cash registers and take note if Eddy or any of his friends left, and notice which way they went. And then I should run through the store until I found Digger and Curtis, or Suzette and Rebecca, and tell them.

Of course, we all knew this wasn't going to happen. Woolworth's is a big store. It's the biggest store in our town, but we all had every aisle memorized, and we knew Reinbach's trio would never be in sections like women's shoes or baby clothes. They'd go right to candy, electronics, and music.

I'd never win by arguing. And Digger made everybody chip in so I could buy two pops while I was waiting. I was surprised that nobody complained. Of course, Rebecca would have given me money anyway. I guessed that Curtis wanted Digger to think highly of him, and maybe Suzette had at last figured out that nobody else liked her very much. So they chipped in.

The last I saw of the heroes before our next Great Catastrophe was their backs as they moved away from the soda fountain. Digger and Curtis, with one walkie talkie tucked under Curtis' jacket in his belt, went in a straight line across the store. Rebecca and Suzette turned right and went in a straight line up the store. Suzette had the walkie talkie under her jacket, which was over her arm.

I would like to present an honest narrative, but I really don't know what happened or how Eddy and his friends did what they did. I've asked the others, but they won't tell me. Even Digger won't tell me.

But as it turned out, I waited for a very long time. I got through one drink and found out I could get a free refill, so I spent the rest of my money on a plate of French fries. I tried to eat them slowly, but I finally finished them, and still nobody came. I'd forgotten my watch, but I was pretty sure that more than an hour had gone by. The lady behind the counter asked me if I was waiting for my parents, and I said I was waiting for my older brother and sister.

I waited and waited. The people in the store thinned out, and I realized it was getting to be supper time. So I knew it had been over an hour. Then I saw all four of them. Suzette had her walkie talkie to her ear, and Curtis had his walkie talkie up at his ear, and they were both talking very fast.

"That is so stupid," I said to nobody. "Now everybody knows they have walkie talkies. And who are they talking to?"

Then I saw that Digger had his winter jacket tied around his waist. And then I noticed that he was walking in his socks.

They came up to the soda fountain, and Curtis and Suzette stopped talking, but they didn't put down their walkie talkies.

Rebecca slammed her purse onto the counter top.

"Do you kids want some pop?" the woman behind the counter asked.

"No!" Curtis exclaimed, and Rebecca quickly added, "No thank you!"

"You should put the radios away!" I told them. "Did Eddy get past us?"

Then Curtis turned to me, and Suzette started a strange, high pitched sound that I didn't recognize at first. Then I realized she was actually whimpering. Real whimpering. She was trying to actually say words, but her voice was so high pitched with suppressed tears that it came out sounding like "meeeny neeny didn't neeny eeny nindy chair."

It sounded so funny that I started to laugh, and then Curt took in a big breath to tell me to stop laughing. But the walkie talkie at his ear didn't move, even when he took his hand off it. The walkie talkie just stayed in place. I realized the awful truth.

"Your radios are stuck to your ears!" I exclaimed.

"The radios are glued to their ears!" Rebecca exclaimed, and then she lifted her hand, palm open, with the purse attached to it, and slapped both down on the countertop. "They used super glue!" I realized that her purse was glued flush against her hand. I stared at Digger.

"They got my shoes," he said.

"Not just your shoes!" Curtis exclaimed.

"They glued a chair in the boys shoe department right before I sat in it," he said to me. "I got stuck by the seat of my pants."

"How'd you get out of it?" I asked.

Digger flashed his blue eyes at me. "How do you think, Jean?"

Suzette was still whimpering. Now it sounded like, "Mamm onna mau my mom an mo mome."

The lady behind the counter said we could all have free pops. Then she went into the back room where the grill was.

"Please tell me how they did it," I asked.

"No!" they all barked at me.

"My grandmother's going to kill me!" Digger exclaimed. "A pair of shoes and a pair of pants!" I realized that he'd left the seat of his pants back in the shoe department.

"At least you don't have a radio stuck to your head!" Curtis snapped.

"Mee ahh to mine a doctor," Suzette whimpered. Rebecca translated: "We have to find a doctor."

"Can a doctor get the super glue off?" I asked.

The counter lady started to come out again, saw all of us sitting there, and went back.

"I think that lady is laughing at us!" Curtis exclaimed, ready to be angry at her hard heartedness.

"No, she feels really bad for you, Curtis," I told him. "She gave you a free drink. But she doesn't want to tell us to finish our pops and leave. And we have to leave."

Digger looked at me, his eyes helpless. In our house, our mom and dad would have laughed off the pants. Maybe we would have gotten a lecture, but I'd never been afraid to go home and tell Mom I'd done something stupid. But to Digger's grandmother, there was no such thing as a small matter. He'd ruined his shoes and torn out the bottom of his trousers. Those were big offenses at his house.

"Come to our house," I told him. "You can get a pair of my Dad's boots and then we can go over to

Miss Harris' house. She's got lots of old clothes she collects for the mission work. Maybe she can give you a pair of pants."

"Mut if me maff to mo to memermency moom?" Suzette whimpered. By now she was snuffling and shedding tears. But she'd given up on pulling on the walkie talkie that was glued to the side of her face. We all looked at Rebecca to translate.

"What if we have to go to the emergency room," Rebecca said. She let out a heavy sigh. "Somebody give me a couple quarters, and let's call Mom."

Mom did have to take Curt, Rebecca, and Suzette to see our doctor. She was sure he could get the glue unstuck for them. She brought along a pair of Dad's old boots for Digger, and on the way to the doctor's she dropped us off at Martha Harris' house.

Martha Harris was as kind as she could be. I didn't dare laugh even then because I really wanted Digger to tell me how Eddy and his friends had done it, but Digger wouldn't talk about it.

In fact, the only thing he told Miss Harris was that he'd sat in his glue and lost his pants and shoes that way. We had hoped she might have old clothes for him, but right away, she said, "Digger, you've done so much work for me, that surely you deserve a new pair of jeans and some shoes."

She got her purse and she gave him several bills. "Go take care of your needs, just like you've taken care of mine, son." And she smiled at him in a way she had that meant she thought something was funny, but endearing as well.

I was really relieved that everything was solved this quickly. But Digger was all choked up by what she said. "Thank you," he said as she put the money in his hand. He could hardly talk. He had to look down, and he stuffed the money into the side pocket of his ruined trousers.

"I'm so proud that you're my friend," she said. "Both of you." And she rested her hand on my head.

Then we hurried away to get to Woolworth's so that Digger could get what he needed. He kept his jacket in place to hide the gaping hole. But the afternoon was above freezing, so it wasn't too bad. I still didn't say anything funny, and I begged him to tell me what had happened, but he wouldn't do it.

We walked all the way back to Woolworth's, and while he was trying on new trousers, I slipped over to boy's shoes. Sure enough, I found one of those cheaply padded chairs where people sit to try on shoes or just to rest. Right in front of it, a pair of shoes was solidly and immovably glued to the floor. And a heart shaped patch of denim that had once been the back side of Digger's old trousers was so firmly glued to the padding of the chair that I couldn't pull it up.

Nobody laughed about what had happened because Curtis and Rebecca wouldn't say how Eddy and his friends had gotten glue on the walkie talkies, or on Rebecca's purse. I suspected from some things that I overheard that there had been some sort of confrontation between Eddy and Suzette and he'd taken away her walkie talkie to tease her with it, passing it to his two cronies. And when she'd snatched it back and put it right to her ear to call Curtis (just to show Eddy how smart she was), it was already glued, and it stuck.

But super gluing something to somebody's skin is no joke. Rebecca came home with her hand bandaged up and sore, and Curtis' skin was sensitive to either the glue or the solvent used to remove it, and he had a burning hot rash on the little square of skin on his cheek where part of the walkie talkie had stuck. His ear seemed okay, because his hair had partly protected the skin there.

I'd thought it was funny at first, but when I saw how much pain the joke caused Rebecca and Curtis, I felt sorry for them. Secretly, I felt like I'd been lucky. I'd gotten two free drinks and a plate of French fries out of it.

Chapter 17: Disaster

On Saturday nobody felt like doing anything. The lake was starting to thaw, and the ice was still good close to the shore, but nobody felt like skating any more. There was slush everywhere on the roads. Mom started out the day saying everybody had to help clean, and we did. But Peter and Noelle kept fussing and crying. And then Curtis was almost as bad, so Rebecca and I ended up doing most of the work, which often happens. Digger called to say he had to help his grandmother that day, and he couldn't go over to Martha Harris's. I knew he was disappointed.

So I was pretty glad to leave just after lunch to work at Miss Harris's. I had to keep an eye open for trouble as I hurried over to her house, but ever since that one bad day, I had never seen the Reinbach gang over that way on a Saturday. And today was no different. But when I reached the house, I saw to my dismay that Mrs. Everett's car was there. It was just going to be that kind of day. I hurried up the slushy driveway, knocked on the door, and then opened it. Some days, she left it unlocked for me.

The house was dead silent. Normally I would have called out, but Mrs. Everett didn't like that, so I pulled off my coat and hurried to the bedroom.

It was empty. There was no sign of Martha Harris and no sign of Mrs. Everett. But her car was there. Then I started calling out loud. I ran upstairs, but there was nobody there. I even looked in the basement, but it was silent.

The phone in the kitchen rang, and I ran and got it. I don't know why, but I started to cry as I picked it up. "Hello?" I asked.

"Jean," my mother's voice said. "Stay there honey. We're coming to get you. Are you all right?"

I was crying. "I can't find Miss Harris," I said.

"She's at the hospital. Mr. Orlando just called. Your father's on his way to get you."

"Mom, is she dead?" I asked. "Did she die?"

"No honey. She's in surgery. Dad's coming."

She didn't want me to hang up until my dad came. Then I got my coat, but he ran up the walk. I was surprised. I think Dad was confused because he picked me right up. He carried me out to the car like I was a little girl. He kept telling me everything was all right. In fact, he reminded me of Digger all of a sudden, but I wasn't sure why.

We have a lady at our church who is an emergency room nurse, Mrs. Crawford. I was surprised, when Dad got me home, to see her there, waiting for me. Digger came in just as I was taking off my coat.

"Let's all sit down," Mrs. Crawford said kindly. She was about Mrs. Everett's age, but Mrs. Crawford was as nice as Mrs. Everett was cross. Digger and I sat next to each other on our long couch and Mrs. Crawford sat down. Dad came in, and he sat down, too.

Mrs. Crawford explained that Martha Harris had suffered a blockage in her intestines. I wasn't sure what intestines are, except that they're connected to the stomach. So Mrs. Crawford said it meant that Miss Harris' digestion had shut down, and she'd become very sick. But the blockage itself was pretty easy for the doctors to remove. Mrs. Crawford hadn't been working when Mrs. Everett had called for an ambulance, but after Mom had called her, she'd phoned in to the hospital to find out what she could. She said it didn't look too bad, overall. Martha would probably get through the surgery, and then after about a week she would be allowed to come home.

"Can I see her soon?" I asked. And Digger nodded.

Mrs. Crawford shot a questioning look at my father.

"When she's able, Jean," Dad said.

"You know," Mrs. Crawford said. "Cancer has a lot of ups and downs, Jean. And Digger. There may be more episodes like this."

"Mom said the church would help her," I said. "Why doesn't the church help her?"

Again, Mrs. Crawford looked at Dad, but Mrs. Crawford wasn't angry. She looked back at me. "You're right," she said. "Every now and then somebody slips through the cracks. But we've got to make sure that doesn't happen again."

"We can take the ups and downs," Digger said. "We're her friends. Both of us. We want to help her like we've been doing. We want to see her."

My mother came in, and Dad nodded.

A kind of light came into Mrs. Crawford's eyes as she looked at Digger. "I want to warn you that dealing with cancer, especially at this stage, can be very difficult. But I think you can face it and help your friend. You should be prepared for the unexpected and then do everything you can to help her and support her."

"They've been doing that very well," Dad said quietly. "I'm proud of both of them."

Digger's eyes were big in his face. He was pale. "Have you ever seen anybody die?"

The question took everybody back, but I was glad he asked it. I wanted to know.

Mrs. Crawford nodded and suddenly smiled. "Yes, and I can say that the death of one righteous person can do more than a hundred sermons. His sheep hear His voice, William. When He calls them home, sometimes I've longed for Him to call me, too.

Because I knew He was calling them, and they could hear Him and wanted to go." She hesitated. "I don't know Martha all that well, but I think, when it's her time, she'll hear Him, and she'll want to go to Him."

She seemed completely convinced, and I felt stronger about it.

"We do grieve about death, children," she told us. "But we don't grieve like people who have no hope."

For a moment everybody was silent, and then I said, "When will she be out of surgery?"

"I called our records department at the hospital," Mrs. Crawford said. "Martha has no next of kin, so your family will be notified of everything. You can call in, or they'll call you. I expect it will be a few more hours."

Dad stood up. "I'll get Pastor and go down," he said.

"Dad, can I go?" I asked him.

He turned to me, shot a glance at Mom, and said, "Not yet, Jean. But I'll find out when you can see her."

198

We could only wait. But I was surprised by Mrs. Crawford. Before she left, she took both Digger and me by the hand. "I've just gone to being part-time at the hospital," she told us. "I'll start to look in on Martha. Thank you for caring for her. I think she has more to give all of us." She smiled at us. "We'll see what the Lord does."

We said goodbye, and for a minute after she left, Digger and I just stood there. "It's like being a grown up," I said after a second.

"Then I'm calling Mr. Orlando," Digger told me. "He knows all about carpentry. We can do a lot while she's in the hospital."

That was how Digger handled it: by working as hard as he could. The next day was Sunday, and Pastor at last announced from the pulpit that Martha was a missionary retired from the field, and she was ill. Better late than never, I thought. But even though I was annoyed at first, once the church people realized her needs, they did pitch in to help.

The ladies' Bucket Brigade took over the house to really give it a good cleaning, and somehow the church managed to buy her a hospital bed. I didn't like it when I saw it, but Mrs. Crawford told me it could elevate and would be helpful in easing pain and reducing congestion. Miss Harris didn't take nearly as many pain killers as she was supposed to. She said she didn't want her senses dulled by them, and she would rather bear the pain and keep her senses keen. After Digger and me, her reluctance to take pain medication annoyed Mrs. Everett more than anything else. Mrs. Everett actually had a lot to say about "accepting the facts," and I didn't understand what this meant.

The next Wednesday night, I was told that I would be allowed to see Martha Harris briefly. Mom told me that she would be on one or two IVs, and she might have a breathing tube, and I shouldn't be startled by those things.

I'm sure that my mother walked into the hospital room with me, but I don't remember her being there. I only remember seeing Martha Harris with her face so pale it was gray. And there were tubes in her.

I came to the bedside, and she opened her eyes. I couldn't move. I was numb.

A light of recognition flickered in her blue eyes. Her voice was quiet from weakness, but she made it reassuring and kind. "It's still me under these tubes," she said. "Don't be afraid, Jean."

She had narrow clear tubes running to her nose, and she had long IV tubes that went right into needles embedded in the back of her hand. I couldn't take my eye off the IV needle when I saw it. To me it looked very big, and it was going right into her hand. Somebody had taped it into place.

"His hands were wounded for me," she said quietly.

I didn't answer her. "The needle doesn't hurt," she told me. "They tape it down so it doesn't move, and it doesn't hurt."

I couldn't talk for a second. "A letter will come for me," she said. "From the translation society. Will you send them a reply and tell them the answer will have to be delayed?"

"Yes." I nodded. But the question brought me back to real life. It reminded me that she would get out of here. Mrs. Crawford had said we had to be prepared for the unexpected. We had to help Martha Harris. I had to stop being afraid of all of this.

"Can I take your hand?" I asked.

"Grasp my fingers." She wiggled her fingers.

I did, and her fingers curled around my hand. Then I felt better.

"Digger misses you," I said. "He wants to see you, too."

"How is he?"

"He's worried about you."

"I pray for him. And for you. Every waking hour. Tell him I miss him. I bet he's working on the house, isn't he?"

I was astonished. "Yes. How did you know?"

A faint, knowing smile played around her lips. I knew that expression. "Because I knew he would use a setback as a chance to do good. Ask him to set up a dartboard for us. We'll play darts."

The nurse came to tell us we had to leave. Martha Harris was so gray and there were so many tubes running in and out of her that I was afraid that if I kissed her I might disturb something. So I only said goodbye.

One of the ladies at church sold vitamins and health supplements, and everybody consulted her about their allergies and lower back pain and things like that. She declared that Martha Harris needed to have all natural fibers in her bedroom. I don't know if she was right or not, but everybody decided to follow her plan, and--with Digger's help--they bargained for a really large piece of cotton fiber Berber carpet. Mr. Orlando installed it, and he showed Digger how to really put down carpet that was wall to wall so that it didn't come up on the edges.

The ladies put up new curtains, and they made up the bed with cotton flannel sheets, cotton blankets, and a down quilt. It was all very pretty when they'd finished. Even with that horrible, mechanical bed.

And Digger understood about the dartboard. "It's because she'll be confined to her bed," he told me. "We'll put it up on the wall across from the foot of her bed, and then we can play darts with her."

Digger had worked as hard as he could, every day after school, to help Mr. Orlando. They'd put in new insulation upstairs, and they'd taken apart the small back deck because some of the boards were rotting out. Then they'd put in new boards. Digger wanted to help because of Miss Harris, but I knew he also wanted to learn how to do things like that. He liked working hard with his hands and with tools. And he really liked working with Mr. Orlando.

But that day, with Miss Harris coming home soon and so much good work done, Digger seemed unhappy.

"What's wrong?" I asked him. "She really will come home, Digger. We'll get to see her again."

"My grandmother doesn't like all the time I'm spending here," he said. "She says she doesn't think I'm working over here like I tell her I am."

I let out my breath. Digger's grandmother is one of those people who never misses church, but her face would split if she ever cracked a smile. She wanted people to think she was a good Christian, and she certainly lived a tidy, organized, orderly life. But she had no sympathy for real people. Not even for Digger.

"Did she say anything about sending you away?" I asked.

"She never comes out and says it," he told me. "She just asks me why she should keep me with her if I'm determined to go out and waste my time hanging around an old house."

"You've been coming over here every Saturday for weeks," I told him. "She's never complained about it before."

He hesitated. Then he said, "I know this is going to sound stupid. But my grandmother gets jealous."

"What?" I was amazed.

"She acts like I'm nothing but trouble, but if I start to pay a lot of attention to anybody else or get really happy about something, she starts to act like I'm not spending enough time at home." He was suddenly disgusted. "Half the time she acts like she wants me out of the house unless I'm actually doing something that she wants done. The other half of the time she acts like I owe it to her to be at home, even if I'm just sitting there." He saw my face, and he said,

"I'm sorry Jean. I can't make you understand. You have a happy family."

"Does she love you?" I asked.

"I don't know."

"Miss Harris thinks your great. She told me she knew you'd be doing good while she was in the hospital."

He brightened on that.

I knew he didn't want to get sent back to his real home. "We'll have to pray about it." I said it without thinking.

"Now you sound like Martha Harris. Okay." He nodded at me and glanced at the door. "Thank you. Let's see if Mr. Orlando knows where we can find a dart board."

Miss Harris came home a week after she went into the hospital. She was still very weak, and we weren't allowed to see her until the next Monday. By then she didn't have any tubes in her any more. And she actually looked so much better that it seemed to me that she looked well.

She wanted to see me at her best, and so my mother picked me up from school right after lunch and drove me over. We could still see her only one at a time, so Digger would come later.

Mr. Orlando was there, still finishing up the back deck. Other people had been in and out. The house looked brighter and fresher now. I liked the sound of people coming and going, and I think that Martha Harris did, too.

Mom went to the kitchen to make tea for us and coffee for Mr. Orlando. I went into the front bedroom, and Martha was in her new bed, sitting up, with her Bible on her lap. She opened her arms to me, and I wanted to run to her, but I was afraid she might still be hurting.

"Are you in pain?" I asked.

"Oh, I'm always in pain. It's such a nuisance. Come here on this side."

So I did, and she took me into her arms and kissed me. "I missed you, my bright jewel. Were you afraid?"

"Yes," I told her. "I was afraid the whole time. And I missed you. But now you're home. Do you like what we've done?" I threw my glance at the room.

She nodded. "Very much. And I missed you, too. I'll be here for a while longer."

"Will you be able to walk around again?" I asked.

"I think so, dear. I'm still recovering from the surgery, but once that's healed, I should be all right for a while." She stroked my cheek, and her eyes were suddenly serious. "Until the next crisis." And she looked at me, to see if I understood.

I nodded. "Okay."

"Sit alongside me," she said. So I kicked off my shoes and scrambled up alongside her, in the crook of her arm. She showed me where she was in her Bible reading, and she drew one of the squiggly Greek words for me. "Arche," I said right away.

"Oh, very good. What's this?" And she wrote out another.

"Logos! The Word!"

"You've got an excellent memory, Jean Anderson. Try this."

"Theos!" And then I said it all for her: "En arche en logos kai logos en pros theos! In the beginning was the word, and the word was with God!" I looked up at her and beamed happily.

She smiled down at me. "We'll have to find some challenges for you."

Then we looked up. Mom and Mr. Orlando were standing in the doorway. Mom was bringing us tea. There was an odd light in her eyes as she looked at me, like she was seeing me for the first time.

Mr. Orlando was a short, stocky man with broad shoulders and jet black hair that grew like a thick ruff of fur on his head. He also had jet black eyebrows that were as thick as heavy crayons.

"Well I'm impressed," he said as he came in with his coffee. "But it's all Greek to me!"

For a few minutes he talked about the work he was doing. Then he finished his coffee and went out to get back to it. We had our tea, and I offered to take the things out to the kitchen.

I put everything by the sink, and then I opened the back door where Mr. Orlando was working.

"Hullo, Jean," he said. He was bent over one of the new boards on the deck. "Everything all right? Come to watch?"

"Do you like working with Digger?"

"Sure," he said. "Nice boy. Hard worker. He wants to learn how to do this type of work. Always nice to see."

Mr. Orlando was our head deacon at church. He had once told me it was his job to help everybody. So I told him about Digger. He didn't rebuke me for telling him exactly what I thought. When I was finished, he said, "Every now and then the church gives a Christian citizenship award to a young person. I'll see what I can do."

"Do you think that will change his grandmother's mind?"

"I can't say for sure. But I do know that the pastor's good opinion is really important to---to some people. If he has a high opinion of Bill (that was

Digger), it might give Mrs. Riley a better reason to keep him with her."

I nodded. I knew he didn't want to say anything bad about Mrs. Riley, Digger's grandmother, but he also wanted me to know that he understood that Digger needed a really strong advocate to convince her to keep him.

"Some people need incentive and encouragement to do the right thing," he told me at last. "It does take a lot of courage for an elderly woman to raise a teenage boy. She'll probably feel better if she feels like the men in the church want to help her."

"Thank you, Mr. Orlando," I said.

"You got a heart of gold, Jean," he told me. "So does young Bill. I'm glad I can help you."

Chapter 18: A Glimpse of Heaven

The next Sunday at church, I noticed Mr. Orlando whispering to Pastor and giving a quick jerk of his head to Digger and Digger's grandmother as they walked into the sanctuary. Both men spoke with each other, and Pastor pulled out a slip of paper from his pocket and a stub of pencil and jotted some things down.

During the announcements before the sermon, Pastor said that the head of the deacon board had recommended a young person for the Christian Service Award. He launched into a short but glowing speech about a young man who had given up many Saturdays to work for the church in ministering to the needs of the sick and shut-in. Then he called Digger up to the platform (though he called him William) and presented him with a tiny lapel pin of a gold cross. Everybody said "Amen!" as Digger, surprised and red-faced, accepted the award and shook hands with Pastor. I glanced at Mrs. Riley. Her expression hadn't changed much. I think she was surprised, too. She didn't look angry or perplexed, only very calm and tranquil, as she always looks at church. Maybe I've been hard on Digger's grandmother. She's not a woman who raises her voice or uses bad words. She always stays quiet and calm, even when she says things that make Digger feel like she might send him back to his parents.

Digger, still red-faced, went back to his place next to her, and she accepted this with her usual calm reserve. But several of the men around him patted him on the back and told her she had a lot to be proud of. She nodded at this and did her best to smile. Then Mr. Orlando stood up to have the ushers come forward, and he stopped to give more glowing words about Digger. He talked about the two of them working on Miss Harris's house and said that Digger loved to work with his hands and was an excellent pupil. Then he talked about the church's constant need for men who could give their time to helping the widows, single ladies, and infirm people with household repairs and work.

After the service, more of the people shook Digger's hand, and several told his grandmother that he was a very fine boy and a model to the youth group. She was always very polite, and she nodded and

214

smiled and said thank you. Digger caught my eye as I went with Rebecca to get Peter and Noelle from children's church. We exchanged looks for a moment, and then he smiled very faintly, as though he thought maybe I'd had something to do with this, or had at least known about it.

But from that Sunday, Mr. Orlando called around to Digger's grandmother once a week to update her on work at the Harris house. And when ever he was running down to the hardware store on errands for the church, he would pick up Digger, and they would go together.

Digger didn't talk about the award much, and I realized that his grandmother had been nice about it but hadn't made a big fuss about it like my parents would have done. But talk of not being able to raise Digger and her comments that he was simply hanging out at the Harris house on Saturdays stopped.

Miss Harris did get better from her surgery. She was able to walk around within another week, and she even worked on the translation project for several hours every day. Somewhere in there, she asked Digger and me to call her Martha, and we did. After all, "Miss Harris" wasn't really correct, because she was actually "Dr. Harris," but that was too formal. So we called her by her first name.

In the mornings she was strongest and best able to cope with her pain, so she did as much as she could while the sun was traveling up in the sky. But as afternoon approached, she would become more uncomfortable and tired, and she would usually retreat to the sofa to rest and read. On bad days, she would have to go to her bed.

I found out that I could take our school bus to her house if Mom gave me a written permission, so on Wednesdays I would go over there right from school, and Dad would pick me up after Wednesday night church.

But some Wednesdays, Mrs. Everett was there, and even though she took good care of Martha, she seemed to get more and more cross with her for not taking her pain medication. I learned how to help Martha get comfortable. I would make her mint tea, and there was an insulated hot pack that I dropped in a big pan of boiling water and then wrapped in towels. I would put this on Martha's feet as she was lying down and wrap them snuggly together, and this seemed to make her feel better. We worked out a routine for fighting pain. Martha told me that a lot of battling pain is actually mental, so if you figure out a routine, then your mind will start to tell your body that the pain is not as severe even while you're still going through the routine. As soon as she heard the kettle whistle, she would feel more able to deal with the pain.

Mrs. Everett didn't like any of this, and she didn't like me. She always told me I would spill the tea on Martha or that I was making a mess or being too noisy. One day she told me that if I would leave Martha alone, Martha would take the pain medicine and be able to sleep better. I asked Martha about this, and Martha said it wasn't true.

Later, when I was in the kitchen washing up, Mrs. Everett came in and told me I was a sneaky little girl, because I'd carried what she said back to Martha.

"No you're sneaky!" I said to her. "You say things about Martha when she can't hear you. That's what a sneak does!"

She started to scold me about how little I understood cancer and sickness, and I yelled, "I understand Martha, and I want her to do what she thinks is best. Not what you think is best!"

Then Martha called me. So I turned off the water and went to the bedroom. Martha told me to apologize to Mrs. Everett, and I did. After Mrs. Everett walked out, Martha asked me why I raised my voice at her, and I told her everything. After that, Mrs. Everett came less, and Mrs. Crawford came more.

Sometimes Digger was allowed to take the school bus with me over to Martha's house. As spring came, she began to feel better and better, and so on Fridays we would go over to see her and have supper with her and play Scrabble or Risk, and then my Dad would pick us up.

She could always beat us at Scrabble. She was the best Scrabble player I'd ever seen. She would lie on the sofa and look at the board on the floor, where we sat, and she would pass her letters down to me and show me where to put them. Sometimes she would let us play a game with each other and she would watch, or fall asleep.

One night while we were playing, and she had fallen asleep, I heard her make a strange sound. Digger and I both looked up. She was on the sofa, and her mouth had fallen open, and she was making a kind of sound that seemed almost musical at first, like a faint singing without words. Then I realized that she was making the sound from pain. It was like a tearless crying in her sleep. Digger and I both stood up and looked at her. The sound went on. I had laughed at Suzette's odd whimpering, but this was real. It was horrible.

"Wake her up, Jean," Digger whispered. "She's in pain!"

"Digger, if I wake her up, then she'll know she's in pain. At least now she's not really conscious of it. Not all of her, anyway."

But just then Martha opened her eyes. She saw us looking down at her, both of us looking very frightened.

"What is it, children?" she asked. "What's wrong?"

"You were groaning in your sleep," Digger said.

"Yes, I'm uncomfortable. Don't be frightened."

"Please," Digger began with a glance at the door of her bedroom where the pain pills were kept. "Don't you think--"

"Son, I took one," Martha said. "I must at least wait until midnight to take another or else--call the nurse if I must." She spoke with catches in her breath. "Anything stronger has to come by an injection."

"Maybe we should get Mrs. Everett over here early," I said. She was due to come at eleven anyway.

Martha looked at me. "She can't change it," she said. "This is what happens--the pain is severe."

Her eyes flicked from me to Digger. "If--you're frightened--you need not--stay--"

"I'll stay," I said. Digger gave a jerk of his head for a nod.

We lost her again to another battle of sighs against the pain. Sweat shone on her face.

"Is this really normal?" Digger asked, and she nodded.

"Children," she said at last. We both looked at her. "The only thing left is morphine. I won't take it. I want to keep my mind. I want to stay fully conscious and aware."

"Why?" I asked her. "Can you tell us?"

"In Africa. The Christians suffered." She took in a great breath, and her eyes became clearer and more determined. "Their medical conditions weren't good, and many of them died without medication or pain killers. Those are my people, O God," she said. But she stopped herself. She became calmer.

"Should we help you sit up?" Digger asked. She nodded, and we helped her up.

She told us the rest. "It was common for the country people who were Christians to see heaven before they died. They said they were in fellowship with Christ the Son in their sufferings. It was another way to more fully know Christ the Son." She looked at Digger and then at me, her eyes weary. "Over there, the people seem to understand that calling better than they do here."

"Is it a sin to take pain medicine?" I asked her.

She shook her head. "Some people have to. Not everybody who is in pain has this calling, Jean. But I want it. I want to see heaven like they did."

"You will," Digger told her. "You'll go there."

"I want the final triumph over the flesh in this life. I want to testify of seeing the walls of heaven, if God will hear that prayer." And then her eyes filled up with tears.

"Then we'll help you," Digger said, his voice calm. "If you're not afraid of being in pain, we won't be afraid."

"Children, this is very personal. Something that's a part of my walk with God," she said. "Will you keep it confidential? I don't want others to be judged by my choices, and I don't want to be judged by others."

We both nodded, and then I said, deliberately and clearly, "I'll keep it between us," and Digger said, "So will I."

She became very quiet, and I saw a kind of gentle light come into her eyes. The pain seemed to leave her for a moment. She rested her hands on us, one hand alongside each of our faces. "The Hall of Heroes," she said quietly. "Is here."

Chapter 19: Heroes Triumphant

 Spring broke through at last. I know that in other books and poems Spring is a glorious, blossomy sort of thing. Where I live, Spring always starts out very soggy. Soggy and muddy. The piles of snow dwindle into grimy, forlorn trailers and spindles. These seep into the ground and make mud.

But life wakes up. The branches put out little buds, still waiting for warmer days. The air gets softer and gentler, and you can go bare headed without your ears stinging. If you have lots of old clothes and comfortable boots, early spring is interesting. You just have to get over any fear of getting muddy and wet.

Curtis spotted an old rowboat stuck in the marshes on the other side of the lake, and he wanted us to get it and claim it for ourselves or return it to its rightful owners and maybe get a reward for bringing it back.

At first, he and Digger were going to go after it, but then Rebecca said she wanted to go, and Digger invited me to come along so I wouldn't feel left out. But then when it was the four of us, Rebecca said she ought to ask Suzette or Suzette would think we didn't like her. Curtis, Digger, and I didn't like Suzette, but we didn't complain that much because it was a cinch Suzette would never want to slog through the mud to get into the marsh.

But we'd miscalculated. Suzette said she would be right over, and she came right away. No waiting around this time. To her credit, I will say that Suzette didn't try to blame Digger or Curtis for having a walkie talkie glued to her head. She'd made a big fuss about it, and she'd cried and whimpered about it more than the others, but I think maybe it had really scared her. After the doctor had gotten it off, her skin was raw, too, but she never complained about that, either.

I was ready to give her another chance, but as the rest of us went into the laundry room of our house to get our boots and old things on for going into the marsh, she said, "Is Jean coming? Doesn't she have to go over to that lady's house?"

Right then I decided that once you're Suzette, you're always Suzette, but Digger said, "That's not until this afternoon."

Then she smiled at me and said, "I just didn't want you to be late and get in trouble." But I think she knew she'd annoyed Digger.

We trudged out to the marsh. It was a little past eight in the morning, and the air was fresh and clean. Curtis led the way. We went around the lake, and then he found one of our favorite paths into the marsh. It was solid footing for a good way, and then the ground got spongy, and we had to move from one little clump of solid earth to the next. That's the challenge of a marsh. Thick, reedy grasses grow everywhere, and the footing might look good, but then you step down and sink into mud up to your hip. Curtis and Digger and I went through a couple times, but if you go through, the others pull you out.

It just takes a lot of time to travel any distance. Curtis kept getting his bearings again and trying to direct us to where he thought the rowboat would be.

But the ground was getting more and more watery. We came up to long, shallow pools of water.

"I think it's too far into the lake for us to get to it on foot," Digger said at last.

"But when I saw it, it had its stern pushed up, like it was on some kind of solid ground," Curt said.

Rebecca glanced around. "Maybe we should go further around the lake and come in from a different angle."

We were all interested now. We voted on her plan, and so we backtracked to solid ground and walked further around the lake, then went into the marsh again.

By now it was nearly ten. We pushed through the reeds and soon found boggy ground again, but then Digger found a kind of island in the marsh: solid earth that was like a ramp right through the marsh. The reeds grew thickly here, but there were also one or two stunted and emaciated little trees.

We heard music then: music and static, like from a radio. And we smelled smoke. All of us got really quiet, and I think we all had the same thought at once. Just as we looked at each other, we clearly heard a voice: a teenage boy.

Nobody said a word, and then Digger gave a jerk of his head towards the music and the voice, and we all followed him, dead silent, in single file.

We were on some kind of promontory that jutted into the marsh. More trees appeared, not very big, and then we saw, through the reeds, the familiar shape and color of our clubhouse. Everybody got down on all fours in the grass.

We heard somebody say, "They're in the back under the pile!"

And then a question that we couldn't hear distinctly, and the same voice, "No, it's teriyaki flavored. Let me!"

Digger and Curtis were in front, and they scrambled forward. As they pushed aside the grasses, I saw somebody---I think it was Eddy Reinbach---duck inside the clubhouse. He was talking to somebody who was already in there.

Digger suddenly shot out of the grass and Curtis followed. Suzette, Rebecca and I ran after them.

Digger and Curtis slammed the clubhouse doors closed, and Rebecca raced to the very best thing she could have found: a long chain with a padlock coiled up on the ground. It was what they used to lock up their plunder at night.

The whole shed rocked and the boys inside pounded it so hard that I thought they would break through, but I ran to Curtis and helped him push against the door on his side to keep it closed.

"Use your cell phone!" Digger shouted at Suzette. "Call the police! Call Officer Franks!"

Rebecca closed the latch. She slipped the padlock through one end of the chain and padlocked the latch. Then she ran the chain around the shed, opened the padlock, and slipped it through the other end of the chain.

Suzette dialed up the police and spoke quickly. She got it right, too. She knew exactly where we were.

We all stepped back from the clubhouse and stared at it. It rocked back and forth. They were shouting at us. Digger saw that they'd built a few campfires out here. He picked up a stout branch that one of them had carried in for firewood, and he banged it three times on the wall of the shed.

"Attention! Attention!" he shouted.

For an instant, the voices inside stopped.

Then Eddy's voice said, very distinctly, "Man, you better let us out of here." It would have sounded a lot more intimidating if he hadn't been locked inside our shed.

"I think it's time for a song," Digger said. And then at the top of his voice he bellowed:

"We are the Hall of Heroes
And that is what we are
And when you doublecross us
The Heroes go to War!"

And then he slammed the club into the side of the shed several times so that it set up a really loud reverb.

"I'm not gonna forget this, Riley," Eddy's voice said.

Digger imitated the song leader at church. He waved both arms at us. "Just the ladies!' he said.

Rebecca, Suzette and I sang out:

"We are the Hall of Heroes
And that is what we are
And when you doublecross us
The Heroes go to War!"

And then Digger did the reverb act again on the shed.

In a few minutes, Officer Franks and one of the town's other police officers came pushing through the grass. They had to use bolt cutters to get the lock off, and Eddy and his friends were really mad at us. They acted like they were going to jump on Digger as they came out of the shed, but Digger didn't back up, and it was Eddy who decided not to jump on him. Then Officer Franks told him to settle down.

We'd caught them with a shed full of shoplifted stuff, so there was no use denying anything, even though they tried. We forgot all about the rowboat and called Dad to tell him we'd found the shed.

* * * *

The next good thing that happened was that as spring came, Martha's pain suddenly got less. She explained to Digger and me that the cancer itself was pushing into key nerves, deadening them so that the pain was less severe. It would be only temporary, but it was a rest for her.

We told her about the recapture of our clubhouse, and she laughed and laughed about it. She wanted to know how Digger had made up a song right on the spot.

"It just came to me. I had to sing something," he told her.

With her pain so much better, she wanted to finish an outline for a handbook on field linguistics that she'd developed. When Digger and I came the next Wednesday, she asked us to help her gather the materials. Over the last several months, all of her files had become disorganized as she had hurried to finish the translation work. So we all went into the dining room and rooted through her parents' old china cupboard, which was where Martha kept her file cases.

To help us understand, she explained that over a year ago, she had actually organized her layout of the textbook, so writing up the outline wouldn't be too hard. We only had to find the index cards that she'd used and put them in the correct order.

She had hundreds and hundreds of index cards, all marked with facts, quotes, references, and information. She told me that this is how many people write scholarly books. They make an outline that acts as a road map, and then they find information and put it on index cards, one piece of information per card. They mark each index card in one corner to show which part of the detailed outline that it's talking about.

I understood what she was explaining before Digger did, and I helped her get the index cards arranged while he hunted through them and gave us anything with a heading on it. The textbook already existed in sketchy form if you put together the dozens of index cards with their carefully annotated major and minor headings and bibliographic headings written on them.

Martha typed up the headings on her computer as soon as we had each section put together. She typed one letter at a time, with her index fingers. I copied down the entire outline longhand, so she could enter it faster. But Digger had taken typing that year. I knew he felt bad for not being of more help, but once I had the outline written, he told Martha he could type faster than she could. He said he would enter the outline for her, and she could check it.

"I'm so grateful to both of you," she said.

He held up his hands. For a minute he looked like Mr. Orlando. "What's a hero for?"

"We don't just lock bad guys in sheds," I told her. "We do office work, too."

After I'd made tea for us, and she and I were in the living room on the sofa, listening to Digger rattling away on the computer, she put her arm around me. The sun was coming in through the bedroom window, and it threw one square of light on the far wall of the living room.

"How long will it take to write the textbook?" I asked her.

"I don't know," she said. She kissed the top of my head. "In the summer, Jean, probably mid-summer, the Lord will call me home."

I looked up at her. "It's nothing to be afraid of," she said. "It's really---the rest of it. All the rest."

"The rest of what?" I asked.

"God spoke the creation into existence," she said. "It's all His spoken Word." She hesitated and tried to explain herself. "Now--these days---with what science has shown us. Do they teach you about DNA? In school?"

"Not yet," I said. "But I know what it is. It's something in our cells that tells our bodies how to grow. It's like our blueprints."

"There are four components of DNA: Amino acid building blocks that have long names, but most people just call them A,G,C, and T. They come in two strands and they pair up with each other. And even though A always bonds to G, and C always bonds to T, the bonded pairs can form any pattern up the DNA chain."

"What does that mean?" I asked her.

"It's an alphabet, Jean. Scientists even call it the DNA code. It reflects the great and loving mind that spoke everything into existence. The pairs form groups of three pairs each, called codons. Those are the syllables. Your DNA describes you. When God spoke everything into existence, somehow, implicit in His spoken, creative word, we were also inscribed there."

She stroked back my bangs. "And in the heavens. There are evidences of His Word there. Before astrology ruined everything and made it a system of fortune telling, the constellations were word pictures, not visual pictures. They formed words in the heavens that foretold of God defeating sin on our behalf. No matter where we look, if we understand that God spoke everything into creation, we see that everything carries the echo of being created by His Word."

"But what does that have to do with cancer?" I asked.

She stroked my hair. "I'm a philologist. My journey through life has been to understand His Word. I've explored how truly meaningful the Word of God is." She looked down at me, her face serious. I realized that she was telling me the deepest, truest thing about herself. "I had to learn how to think through the wording of the Scripture. I wanted to catch every shade of His meaning. The more you pull apart the words and look at the meanings, the more you see of God's nature, His love and His power to save us from sin. God made everything. He even made language, and He put it in us."

She hesitated, and I realized that she wasn't sure if I was following her. I wasn't sure either, but I wanted her to say everything. As I looked at her and waited, she said, "but now I know that there is more to see and understand about His majesty and sovereignty than a human being can know while separated from God by the veil of flesh. When the echo of the word that spoke me is uttered---finished--- I'll reside with Him, complete. A word isn't fully meaningful until it's terminated, Jean. I have to go to God to know Him more fully. And my life reaches its full meaning only after it's completed."

I understood that much, and I didn't like it. "I don't want you to go."

She took my tea cup and set it on the table alongside her, and then she held me. "Somewhere in the heavens, a great story is being told, and the syllables that have said you and me into existence are there in the same paragraph. You and I are parts of a great story of triumph, how God has triumphed through us and in us. And as long as that story is being told, we go where it takes us. But we're never all that far apart from each other. Our time together is meaningful. And it becomes more meaningful as time passes, even after we fade away. You have to look past the material world to the bigger world of what it all means."

I didn't say anything, and I don't think she expected me to. Martha Harris was probably the smartest person I'd ever met. And she looked at everything a little differently from everybody else. But she'd done great things. And she knew great things.

She looked down at me. "You're a beautiful word, a beautiful story still being told," she said. "But a word has to let itself be uttered, so let God speak you. He'll show you all His fullness, even when it seems dreadful. Behind it all is a goodness so great that all history has to unfold to make it clearly stated."

"All right," I whispered.

She kissed the top of my head. "You're my dear friend, my bright jewel to show me God's mercy, my treasure. Did I say these things about you, knowing God will vindicate my words, Jean? Or did God declare these things about you from the very beginning, and all these months are just the way it's come to pass?"

"I don't know," I whispered. "When I joined Young Helps, Mr. Orlando said it was from the Lord."

"I'm almost ready to come before God's throne," she told me. "And be with the Living Word that declares our salvation. It's like a completion. It's where we're all going."

It wasn't a conversation that could end right there, and it wasn't a conversation where I could make an answer. But that was all right. For a moment or two she looked down at me and held me, and part of me did feel like it would be all right. I knew it wouldn't be easy, and yet I knew it would be all right.

Then Digger came in with the print out of the outline. He'd done a good job, she said. So we put away the index cards and book materials, and then we got out the Scrabble board and played until it was time to go.

That night as Dad drove us home, he stopped to gas up the car, and while he was at the gas pump, I told Digger that Martha had told me she expected to live until midsummer. I didn't tell him the rest.

"Mr. Orlando said it would be only a few months," he told me. "He said a lot of people who have cancer actually die of pneumonia."

"Does pneumonia hurt?"

He looked at me. "I don't think it could hurt as much as what she's already been through. I think maybe we've seen the worst of her being in pain."

"Maybe," I said, but then I thought, maybe not. But I didn't say it. There was no need to. You never know what's going to happen with cancer.

"I want to help her get through it," he said.

I nodded. "So do I."

"And I want us to help each other." He looked at me. "Like we've been doing."

His face was anxious, and I realized that Digger and I had somehow become good friends. It was a serious thing. "Okay." I nodded. "I want us help each other." I looked at him carefully so he would know that I knew it wasn't a joke.

Dad was coming back from paying at the window. Digger spoke quickly. "Courage is just deciding to take what comes. That's all it is."

"Just like Faith," I said. "Because God says it."

CPSIA information can be obtained
at www.ICGtesting.com
Printed in the USA
LVOW10s1634181217

560168LV00038B/3981/P